Rex Morgan and the
Mysterious Woman

by

Frederick T. Mobley

DORRANCE
PUBLISHING CO
EST. 1920
PITTSBURGH, PENNSYLVANIA 15238

Dorrance Publishing Co
585 Alpha Drive
Suite 103
Pittsburgh, PA 15238
Visit our website at *www.dorrancebookstore.com*

ISBN: 978-1-4809-3505-1
eISBN: 978-1-4809-3528-0

Characters of the mystery
Rex Morgan and the Mysterious Woman

Rex Morgan — A successful private detective, well-qualified in his well-chosen career.

Anne Towers — Known as Peggy Lausanne, is she hiding from someone or from her past? Is Anne Towers her real name or is she someone else?

Captain Hilary — The Berkeley Police Captain, likes to stay informed of what is going on around him, hates being left out or misinformed.

Sgt. Judy Sturgis — Captain Hilary's secretary, has a romantic interest in Rex Morgan.

John Cotter — FBI Director, covering the Oakland County District.

Jan Roberts — ABC News reporter, persistent in getting her story coverage.

Harold Jabots — NBC News Live, news reporter.

Max Guinean — Known as Luke Leprous, tries to maintain a low profile, in seclusion found out to be an assassin.

Samoa's — Rex Morgan's favorite club diner, a luxurious nightclub.

Lt. Ottoman — a police lieutenant in the Berkeley Police Department

59t. Ballenger — a police sergeant in the Berkeley Police Department.

Barry Williamson — A standing Militias Militia member and assassin.

Mitch Miller — Operations Director under FBI Director, John Cotter, turns out to be a "militia mole" and assassin.

Cheryl Nickles — an Assistant District Attorney.

Wayne Melton — Berkeley Police Commissioner.

Jason Coatis — an officer on the Vice Squad, owner of a real nice cottage.

Larry Flippant — Director of Internal Affairs, carries the nickname, **"Headhunter."**

Milton Bradle — the new FBI Director, after John Cotter.

Sgt. Oystermen — a former Militia member, now a detective in the Berkeley Police.

Karl Smears — a Militia informer, within the Berkeley Police precinct.

Andre' Knowles — Anne Towers' attorney.

Militias Militia — the organization Anne Towers embezzled and they are looking for her.

Rex Morgan and the *Mysterious Woman*

Just after a lazy mid-morning breakfast and the dishes cleared away, and a third cup of coffee poured. Rex heard a truck backing-in next door. Going to the window, a Roland's Moving Service van was backed in the driveway and two men were getting out, started unloading and carrying furniture into the house. A warm spring day for it with the grass turning green with the ground drying up and summer coming on. A model Cadillac pulled up to the curb and a young blonde-haired woman stepped out, started talking to the movers and pointing.

Rex decided to go out, meet the new neighbor, and find out who is moving in next door.

"Hello, are you the new neighbor?" Rex inquired. "I am Rex Morgan, next door. Welcome to our community."

"Hi, I'm Peggy Lausanne, thank you for welcoming me." They talked on while the furniture was unloaded and carried inside. She was from Madison, New Jersey, had been an art instructor at a junior high school full-time and an hourly employee at the high school. She needed a change, so she was opening an art gallery. She decided that was what she had wanted to do; she always had a strong interest in art.

"From a toddler to my senior year in high school. I used to draw and some made it to the school exhibition and some to the county fair as part of an art show for which I received a blue ribbon," she said proudly.

"Wow that was great. Did you keep them after you were out of high school?" "Yes they're stored away at my parent's house in West Virginia," she replied.

"You don't have an accent like they do," Rex commented.

"Yes, I know, I've been away too long. I hardly go back home."

"I was born and raised in Maryland, an only child. Do you have any brothers and sisters? I miss not having a brother or sister."

"One sister, she still lives at home while going to college. She is majoring in landscape design," Peggy stated proudly.

"Ah, that's good, I like it when one tries to improve themselves and increase their knowledge. It keeps the brain active and alert and means a better job or career. It shows ambition and that's a great field to go into, is she planning to start her own business someday?"

A month later Rex looking out the window, noticed a van backed up in Peggy's driveway. Two movers were taking big boxes into the house, National Computers written on the side of the boxes. Why would she want high-tech computers in her house? A laptop home computer is understandable: maybe she intends to operate from her house as well as her art galley. Why would she?

One day Rex decided to visit Peggy and see how she was doing, just chat. She welcomed him in for some coffee and to chat for only a few minutes but she had to leave shortly to go to the art gallery. Inside was nice, well-decorated in traditional style, two real nice paintings in the living room and one in the den where they sat and talked.

Rex had told Peggy when she first moved in that he was retired from service, a full-ranked colonel in the army.

"Now that you've retired from the service, what do you do?"

"Oh, I do private detective work for companies, divorce cases, accident reports, etc." At the mention of detective work, Rex noticed a flicker of alarm in her eyes for a brief second, then gone. "Just local stuff," he said.

"I see, the divorce cases must be interesting, exciting. Is it ever dangerous?" she seemed somewhat relieved.

"Very seldom is it dangerous, on occasions, I carry a gun, depending on the severity of the case, never have shot anyone. Divorce cases are sometimes interesting, sometimes humorous, and sometimes boring." He tried to make the job sound simple and routine.

"I can't imagine a job like that as boring. I would think it would be exciting, some cases even spicy," she said grinning.

"Some are exciting and spicy, some are sad, some are downright disgusting and some are boring just sitting and watching with nothing happening," Rex replied smiling. They talked on for another half hour.

"Well, I've enjoyed talking to you and I hate ending this visit, but I have to get to the art gallery. We'll see each other again, I'm sure."

"I don't want to hold you up we'll have to get together for dinner sometime."

"That would be nice, but it would have to be planned sometime, the gallery keeps me busy."

"How about this Friday night, give me a time you could relax after a full busy day."

"Let me check my schedule and I'll get with you, I'll need your phone number."

Giving her his phone number, she could check him out which is why he didn't like anyone having his number. Very clever of her, though. I will have to stay on my toes around her, be wise to her tricks.

"Tell you what, I'm in and out all day checking on messages and calls and cases; so I'll call the art gallery and you can tell me or leave a message, is that okay?"

"Yeah. It will probably be a message with the secretary, I'm sometimes tied up in a meeting or with a customer or out of office?' Peggy answered with a knowing smile. She catches on fast, a quick thinker: she is no dummy.

Back at his house, Rex thought about Peggy making no mention of computers and catching onto him not giving her his phone number. She wanted to check him out and I need to check her out, see what her game is. How can a schoolteacher afford expensive high-tech computers and an art gallery as well a nice house nicely furnished in a nice neighborhood, unless she has a nice inheritance or something to fall back on or someone backing her financially?

Rex Morgan, a former CIA classified field agent and analyst had always had a keen sense when something was not as it seemed or on the level. As a young man approaching middle age, while physically fit, not much fat but more muscle and lean, at the age of 45.

As a young boy growing up, he played coppers and robbers with him being the cop, later he went into reading detective stories, watching the news and reading books on detective work and the FBI. He found the adventures of the FBI more exciting and interesting. For Christmas, his parents bought him a computer to do his studies and legality research courses.

To prepare for a career in the FBI, he enrolled in Yale School of Law and stuck it out four hard years working, studying, and going to class, plus four extra years in social studies and research as well and two years in forensic research.

A graduate of West Point, twelve years of military service with four years in intelligence, he was the one to analyze any foreign information and question prisoners. He had learned about people, their emotions, and how to read them as well read their minds and tell if something was original or fake. He could talk the language of military brass, society elite, or the common laborer, and feel comfortable. He learned this over time. He had 4 years of sociology, shy of a Master's Degree plus his law degree and forensic research degree.

After retiring from the CIA and government work, he moved from Washington D.C. to Berkeley, a college town, Southern California University overlooking San Francisco. He knew a fellow government agent there who could help get him set up in a private detective agency. Rex's military and government experience had helped him in getting started. He was doing well now, thanks to Pat Ballenger.

Rex decided to pay a visit to Peggy's art gallery to set a date for their dinner and evening out and to see her gallery as well. The gallery was a real nice place on a busy street. A lot of high-rise office buildings and businesses. There was a fair variety of prints, etchings, sculptures, and paintings on display. Reasonably low priced to high priced. A nice art gallery and well-laid out. She has this on a teacher's salary only, she said. The art more than likely sold on commission but to get started with such a nice selection surely meant connections somewhere, somehow—knowing the right people, someone with class, and a lot of money.

There is more to Peggy than meets the eye, more than she is letting on, like the feeling that he had back at his house.

Peggy was not in and she had not left a message as to when or time of their evening out, so Rex left to attend to other things...

The next day, he returned to the art gallery to see if she was in, she was in a meeting. Checking with the receptionist, Friday would be fine, at 10 p.m., so Rex made reservations at Samoa's, a plush, candlelight and jazz band club with valet parking in the business district. The club owner, Otis Boswell, used to be a business partner with Rex's uncle, also present owner of a plush club off the thoroughfare. A few miles away. Rex sometimes took his good clients there. Rex knew Peggy would like it; it would be a hit with her.

"Well, how was your day? Busy I suppose?" Rex casually inquired on the way to the club.

"Meetings, yes, business slow, people like the paintings but are scared to turn loose with their money. One man tried to get me to come down on the price on one certain painting but I told him no way, not on that painting! He started to give me a hard time and I ordered him to leave, but he refused. I had to call security on him."

"That's too bad but some people are like that. They just think because you having a gallery, you can just give them whatever they want. They don't think or care about your overhead expenses, they just want it."

"A lot of the paintings are sold on commission," Peggy replied. "How was your day?" shifting the conversation.

"Boring, routine stuff," Rex replied. "A man gambling his check away; taking money to provide food and clothing for his wife, and four kids."

"I hate it when a man does that, that's terrible. They should hang him out to dry!"

"In divorce court when the judge gets through with him, he won't be able to gamble, he won't have the money."

"Good enough for him! I hope he has to go in his underwear and barely has enough to eat and get by!"

"You're being a little hard on him aren't you?" Rex asked laughing.

"A man like that deserves it!" Peggy retorted grinning. Rex agreed.

Arriving at Samoa's the chitchat went on when they were not dancing, the jazz was excellent, a mixture of rock n' roll, slow dancing and relaxing intimate music. The steaks cooked to perfection, and the trimmings, dessert a type of pastry, a perfect evening.

On leaving the club, Rex took her on a sightseeing tour of the plush side of the city and up the steep hill overlooking the city.

"Where are you taking me?" Peggy asked grinning on the way up.

"I'll never tell but it's spooky," Rex teased back. At the edge of the hill overlooking the city, it was a beautiful sight to see with all the bright nightlights.

"Is this where you bring all your lady friends?" she teased.

"Of course," they sat looking at the lights and talking for a couple of hours and went back to Rex's house to watch movies and chat. "Your house is so nice, homey, and cozy." Rex thanked her.

A month later, Rex returned to the art gallery to see Peggy as well as the art gallery. In a separate room from the ones he had seen, there were paintings that were well beyond his income. Maybe these are the ones she said are being selling on commission; or maybe they were on loan, no price on them? He had heard that if you have to ask, you couldn't afford it. Rex was curious.

Peggy was talking to a middle-aged couple with a slight accent, probably discussing price. He decided not to bother her but to look around. He did not see anything out of the ordinary, looked like paintings to go on display and some to be shipped in the backroom. He heard someone coming, he quickly moved back into the showroom.

"Can I help you?" inquired a young woman, nicely dressed, her hair curled.

"No, I'm just looking and admiring these beautiful paintings."

"If I can help you with anything or you need assistance, let me know. I'm Kathy."

"I'm Rex; these paintings are beautiful but a bit out of my budget."

"They are beautiful, they were painted by the 'MASTERS' and most of the others in the other room, as well."

"Yes, I presumed that."

Everything seemed to be on the level, but why was there a feeling that would not leave that something was not, as it seemed? From experience, Rex had learned not to push his suspicions aside, even though there were no grounds or reason here, on the surface anyway. How could Peggy acquire such a beautiful art gallery on a teacher's salary unless she had received a huge inheritance or someone was backing or setting her up as a front? The paintings in this room were well beyond anything he could afford. He would check at the license bureau, he knew Dianna Sawyer who worked there: maybe Peggy Lausanne was the one in charge of the art gallery the license was in someone else's name or an organization? It might be fronted by Peggy but belong to the mob. Peggy did have a license to operate an art gallery and she was bonded. If there was anything to hide, she had seemingly covered all the bases. Rex went home to relax and think this through; he was tired and tensed. Suspecting and finding nothing, Rex suspecting Peggy, it was not that he wanted to find something on her; it is just that things do not add up. He hated suspecting Peggy.

The house next door looked like there was no one at home; he would like to slip into the house for a look around and at those computers if they are still there, even though he did not like breaking and entering, but he had on occasion. The evidence could not be of use as evidence in court or anything connected to it without explaining just how he obtained the evidence and what reason he had for breaking and entering. However, it gave him the knowledge he needed on a case. The bad part was he hated thinking of Peggy this way, he only had his suspicions to go on for now. He made up an excuse and knocked on her door, nobody home, he would come back after dark.

At 9:00 Rex dressed in black so to not be spotted, stepped out the back door, and ran around peeking in Peggy's windows. There was no one home, dark except for a nightlight and no car in the garage. The alarm system detached from the box, the backdoor was a deadbolt, which he unbolted, and slipped inside: He easily and quickly moved from room to room, but no computers. The last room locked, this had to be it. It took a couple of minutes but at last, the tumblers clicked to get inside the locked room.

Once inside, Rex moved quickly to the computers and studied the set-up, very complex, too much for him, it did not take long to see that. It was set up so if anyone messed with it, she would know it. Moving out of the room and relocking the door, he wondered what was in the basement. It was decorated nice for entertaining—the bar, game room, restroom and snack bar. He went back upstairs, closed the door and quickly looked around a last time, went out the back door and bolted the door just as lights turned into the driveway. Rex quickly reattaching the security alarm system, raced back to his house as lights went on in Peggy's house.

In his study, Rex wondered why Peggy would need such high-tech computers and how could she afford them when she used to be a schoolteacher? In the office at the art gallery, he had noticed a couple of computers along the wall, a copy machine, and a shedder. Was the art gallery a front, if so, for what and who? Peggy was a smart intelligent woman. Why would she need this? Like he figured back at the art gallery, maybe she inherited a huge inheritance, but his instinct told him no.

The next morning Rex saw her back out of the driveway and drive off, he grabbed his camera case on instinct and rushed out the door to his car to follow her. In a few minutes he saw her car five cars ahead, he continued to stay behind, keeping her in sight. Driving to the parking lot behind the art gallery a garage door went up long enough for her to drive inside and then it went down, but Rex got the license plate number. He could trace that.

At the police station, Rex asked Sergeant Judy Sturgis to speak to Captain Hilary. Rex expressed a desire to trace a license plate number. "And while I'm at it, I'd like to trace yours too" Rex teased.

"Oh you don't have to trace mine, I'll give you my address and phone number too," she replied, grinning. Captain Hilary came to the door of his office. "Okay, Rex Morgan, what have you got? Quit flirting with my secretary, that's my job."

"You jealous, Captain?"

"Yes I am; what have you got?" Rex looking at Sergeant Judy, she grinned.

"Captain, it may be nothing, but the circumstances look suspicious, things don't add up right. I need to trace a license plate number."

"Okay, come on in and tell me the whole story and I want to hear it all, not half the truth but the whole truth, all of it."

Rex laid out the story of Peggy claiming to have retired from teaching school and opening an art gallery but the paintings go from reasonably low priced to more than I make in a year (Hilary listening intently now), the paintings, prints, etchings and sculptures. Then Rex told about the computers.

"Are you, Rex Morgan, saying you broke and entered her house to look at those computers?" Hilary asked, alarmed.

"Now Captain. I didn't say that I broke and entered her house. If I did do that do you think I'd admit it?"

"No, but how do you know that they are complex then?" Hilary asked, suspiciously.

"That is confidential, Captain. I for one thing know the name National Computers, written on the side of the boxes, are a high-tech computer company. The movers carried them into the house. Moreover, when a private detective is on a case, he does not spill guts or he would not be in business very long!"

"Okay, okay, you may or may not be telling the whole story which I figure you're not, but I don't know, but you have stumbled onto something. As you uncover new facts, I want to know, and I want you to keep me informed, that is an order! You and I do not know each other that well yet, but I know you well enough to know that you do not always tell me the entire story. I will run this license number for you, but keep me informed, do not play me! I think you know how I feel about that."

"Yes, I know and I don't intentionally do that, but I know some who would."

"So do I, so do I."

The next day, Sergeant Judy called Rex to say the captain was in a meeting and could not call, but the license number does not exist and nothing found as far as the name, apparently; she lived a good life but the name is a fake. The captain ran the license number and name nationwide, and Interpol as well but nothing came up. "She's a fake," Judy teased.

"Yeah, right, she's a good girl. Ha-ha," Judy mockingly replied to Rex's vague suggestion; maybe Peggy might not even have a police record, and is a good person. "Maybe she's good at what she does, maybe? The license plate should be easy to trace."

"Don't be jealous now, are you a good person?"

"But of course I'm a good person and you'll find that out if you ever take me out, you'll find out."

"Are you asking me to take you out?"

"Well, I'm thinking that's the only way you'll take me out, I'm not the 'Miss Penny' in the James Bond movies if you would have noticed."

"Oh I have noticed you on more than one occasion."

"You have? Well. I'm surprised."

"Oh Kathy, I'm hurt," Rex playfully replied.

"Yeah, right," Kathy said laughing. "You didn't say anything."

"True, I'm sorry."

"Should I believe that?" Kathy laughed.

"Yes, of course," Rex replied, Kathy still laughing.

Checking back with the licensing bureau on the art gallery, they confirmed Peggy's license and her name. Rex drove to the art gallery and waited a distance from the parking lot, his Minolta MO Maximum camera and GOO mm telescopic lens ready. Sure enough, the garage door went up and Peggy came out whipping into traffic. Rex was able to get another picture of the car and the license but not her.

He quickly pulled into traffic and spotted Peggy in about three minutes as she quickly parked on a busy street and went into Woolham's Department Store. Rex finally found a parking space and saw her purchasing a broad grey hat, then going out the back door and into Kerr's Penny Store across the alley, she went out the front door and hailed a cab. By the time Rex found one, she was already gone. She had taken deliberate steps to lose anyone trying to follow her, but why is she hiding and from whom? Had she spotted Rex? If she had, she did a good job of losing him. Where is she going that she did not want anybody following her and for what reason?

Rex ran back to his car and started looking for her only to see her going the other way in her own car. Ha managed to turn around at the next block, but she was gone, the traffic holding him back; she had managed to get back to her own car and lose him. She was good; she was a fast one for sure!

The following day, he waited at a more secluded spot a distance away from the art gallery parking lot until she came out and headed north. Rex with his camera followed at a distance into a rough neighborhood. She turned into a driveway of a crumbling run down tri-level, the shades pulled. She went to the front door and knocked, Rex getting her picture.

A rough-looking, unshaven guy with his T-shirt hanging out on one side and hair uncombed, came to the door and they talked as Rex took their picture twice, she went inside for an hour and came out. While they were inside, Rex took a picture of just the house and then the house and yard. What business did she have with this character? From there she went home.

Getting the pictures developed and then going to see Captain Hilary, Rex brought him up to date on Peggy and gave him the address of the character she went to see and gave Captain Hilary the pictures.

"With this picture and his address, we'll see if we can get a rundown on him, if we have anything on him," Hilary stated. "He looks like bad company."

For a month, things were normal, routine, go to the art gallery, and come home. Surveillance placed on the rough looking character, where he went and when, if anyone came to his house that never happened; a conference-seminar in police technology, forensics, new advanced photography and private detective work was coming up the next month. Rex hated to leave in case something turned up but he needed the latest techniques and knowledge.

Maybe he could talk Borg Bengal, a former partner in his own PI practice now, to watch "Miss Peggy." It would not be free, but Borg owed Rex a big favor. Rex had saved Borg from blowing a case, so he called and right away, Borg knew Rex wanted a favor, he never called otherwise.

"Yes Rex, I remember you: you saved my butt in the Sullivan-Miamian case. I wondered when you would call. If I do you this favor you are asking, it will clean the slate between us, and you will pay my expenses. Okay, I will do it. If I have any suspicions or questions I call Captain Hilary, right. Okay, I'll do it."

Borg had bungled the supposed-to-be evidence in the supposedly air tight case, the authorities thought. Rex reviewing it discovered the fake evidence to throw the police off course and get the case thrown out of court. Upon this discovery, the police were able to pursue the case and convict the suspects. A well-built case until you started looking at it in depth intently and thoroughly checking out the hidden details. Borg owed Rex a big favor now whenever he needed one. Rex needed to revisit the art gallery to see if anything had happened or developed. He felt Borg needed to go along to see the location and layout of the place. He called Borg and expressed his feeling and Borg agreed, he wanted to do this case justice, the right way and prove he could clear his image as a PI. He needed to prove to Rex and the police captain that he was not a complete failure.

In the room of medium to expensive paintings, Rex discreetly pointed Peggy out, talking intently, arguing in a low voice with an Arabic or Mid-Eastern looking man, in his mid-forties, slim but well built. They seemed to be arguing over the price of a painting but there was no painting in that corner or area. Rex got a quick good look at the person and then moved to the next room with Borg. They had not noticed Rex or Borg.

Kathy was there to greet them and try to interest them in a painting.

"The ones that interest me would cost me my annual income or more," Rex stated.

"You can charge it on any major credit card, or put it in layaway. Besides I bet you have a lot of money."

"What gives you that idea?" Rex inquired with a smile.

"Oh, you look the type and you've been here a couple of times now. I figure you have your eye on one," Kathy replied.

"Thank you but you're mistaken. I have to work for a living," Rex replied smiling. "Maybe later I'll buy something but the two people in the other room seem to be having a very serious intense discussion."

"Yeah, that guy keeps trying to get Miss Lausanne to reduce her prices, forgetting that there are overhead expenses and a lot of the paintings are sold on a commission." They talked awhile longer. Rex trying to find out if she had worked for Miss Lausanne very long, if she had known her long. Kathy asked why he was asking, looking at Rex curiously.

"When I buy an expensive painting, I like to know a little bit about the gallery and its owner." "Then you need to talk to Miss Lausanne."

Borg spoke up then and said there is a painting that interested him in the room they had just left. They went back to the other room and while Borg and Kathy debated price on a medium-priced painting Rex discreetly observed the Arabic, self-confident and determined type of person. They were talking too low for Rex to hear whatever they were arguing. After a few minutes, Kathy and Burg reached an agreement on the price, Borg charged it to Master Card. Peggy finally noticed Rex and Borg, said something to the Arab, and walked over to Rex, the Arab turning his back to them and then leaving in a huff, his face turned away from Rex and the others.

"You brought me a customer?"

"Yeah, my friend, Borg Bengal, needs a painting for his living room," Rex introducing Borg to Peggy and Kathy. "You said business was slow so I brought you a customer and I wanted to see you again."

"Oh you're sweet, thank you," then throwing her arms around Rex's neck, she kissed him.

"Should I leave and come back later, go browsing and looking at other paintings or go in the other room for a while?" Borg asked with a smile.

"No, did you see something you like and interesting to you?" Peggy asked quickly turning loose of Rex.

"Yeah this one here I like, rich in color and well-painted," Borg said pointing to a medium size, medium-priced painting.

"A good choice, a nice painting of a beautiful island inlet cove called, The Island Paradise."

Back in the car, Borg explained that he thought it a good idea to buy a painting and see where the charge goes, and he liked the painting anyway. Rex agreed the painting was a beauty and priced right too.

"Good thinking, Borg." It was all set. Borg would stay in Rex's house and watch Peggy while Rex was away at the week and half conference-seminar. It seemed simple enough, easy and routine, hopefully. Rex realized that is when they pull a slick one on you, slick and fast, which Peggy had proven she was more than capable of doing. Rex warned Borg that Peggy was smooth and cunning, she seemed harmless but looks can be deceiving, especially with her!

"She is cagey, a smooth fast operator with cunning that beats anything I've seen, she's a quick thinker and faster than lightning! You will see for yourself, if you take her on! She has outwitted me once or twice, leaving me like no one I've seen!"

"You make her sound like a real slick con-artist, the way you talk, she might be too much for me," Borg said nervously, Rex nervous as well at leaving Borg in charge.

"Wait until you have to track and follow her, she got away from me. Be ready to move at an instant's notice if she goes anywhere. Just watch her house from inside my house and if anyone comes to her house record his or her license plate number only if you can see it, do not let him or her see you! If she leaves, follow her from a few cars back and record where she goes and what she does, just do not let her spot you! I do not want her to get wise to me or get spooked into fleeing! I want to hang onto her! Remember that, whatever you do, remember that," Rex stated, continuing lecturing Borg sternly.

"Okay, I'll keep that in mind but if she is as good as you say? then I will do my best. However. I have never been outsmarted by a woman yet, not that it can't happen." Rex laughed at that, shaking his head and looking at Borg mockingly.

"This is no ordinary woman, you are in for the surprise of your life, you've probably never gone against a woman like Peggy. I do not know if I chose the right man or not. I have the feeling she is going to shame you bad! If you botch this, you can forget about me helping you again! Do you understand that?" Rex stated flatly. "Don't think for a second that you'll be able to pass this off or live it down if you botch this! Doing this right might help you to make things right and give you new experience."

"Yes, I understand that and I will try to do my very best," Borg nervously replied, stressed. Why allow myself to get into this ordeal, he wondered, why did I?

"Captain Hilary knows all about this case up to now and he's dead set against me asking you to cover for me, so if this goes sour and she's spooked he'll be mad at you as well as I!" Rex declared. "He'll come down on you like hellfire!"

"Captain Hilary is in on this too, oh great. I'm really screwed for sure now," Borg declared, shaken, feeling a real bad migraine coming on. "If I had known this, I don't know if I would do this or not."

A week went by, Borg watching and following at a distance of five cars back, he managed to get a close-up picture of Peggy's face with his Cannon 400 and telescopic lens. Maybe this is going to work out smoothly, he thought. Maybe?

Borg took the picture of Peggy to the police precinct, personally to Captain Hilary. Both the captain and Rex were firm about that, the captain said he would get right on it. He could not come up with a match in police files, faxed it to the FBI, CIA and Interpol, but they did not have anything either. However, using the Forensic Facial Profiler, the FBI with help from the CIA was able to match her face with the outline of a woman suspect caught up in an embezzlement case that had leaked out, involving a political extremist right wing organization, the Militias Militia. The word was out to find her!

The organization did not file charges because of their funds in millions of dollars unaccounted for with the federal and state government, which they had not declared. They did not want attention drawn to them, their activities and their organization: and they did not want the Internal Revenue looking at their books and files, the millions of dollars had disappeared and so had she.

The Federal Treasury Department traced the money to Swiss Bank accounts, only some unknown source had withdrawn it and transferred it to Des Moines State Bank; and then transferred to Peru National Bank before they could investigate. The money withdrawn and all the accounts had closed. The mysterious woman and two men whom the federal government suspected owned the accounts or acted for someone who did own the money disappeared after the transfers of the money. The Swiss Bank manager claimed she was an older professionally dressed looking woman with silver-grey hair who closed the accounts and she wore shades the entire time. She could have dyed her hair but he could not say for sure. It might have been Peggy.

The two men were about middle age; one was slim but strong-arm type, dark eyes, not much of any expression, a sort of blank stare or look. The other man was stocky built, big arms, a confident look and blue-grey eyes. Both men wore nice suits. The three of them never said a word to each other the entire time.

The organization claimed they discovered the fake identity after they discovered the embezzlement and she had disappeared. They discovered the Swiss bank accounts but they had already closed; they had not filed charges because they had not finished their investigation they claimed, and it was an embarrassment to their organization. They had trusted her. If they could recover the money, they would prefer to cover it up to save face, without publicity. They had never filed any charges.

This Peggy Lausanne's picture and name, the FBI doubted it was her real name, but faxed it around the country and to Interpol, but they had nothing on her. A dead end unless something turned up in the U.S.

Interpol had heard of the extremist organization, Militias Militia, but not enough to check on. The federal government asked from where did they move and operate. Interpol said they would have to check on that and get back with them on that if they had anything.

The beginning of the second week, Borg had what he thought was a lead out of town. He saw Peggy put two suitcases into the trunk of her car, shut it and went back inside the house for a minute, come out, lock the door and took off in her car headed out of town. Borg followed her at a distance to the town of Palo Alto and watched as she checked in at the Palo Alto Hotel. After she had headed for her room, Borg checked in and noted her room number and name, Linda Guardable. Borg sat in the lobby, waiting for her to come down watching the backside door as well. She stayed in her room and ordered room service instead.

Night came, and it was getting late, at 1:00 a.m., Borg decided to go up to his room, next to hers and listen. Falling asleep in the relaxing recliner, he awoke the next morning. He quickly went down to the checkout desk to find she had checked out at 4:11 that morning. She had given him the slip, just as Rex said she would do. He would go back to Berkeley outsmarted by a woman! No wonder he didn't get many cases like Rex did! Maybe she went back home, but why did she come here, to get rid of him for some unknown reason? Had she detected him watching and following her? Rex said she is a smooth and quick operator and thinker. Here it is 9:00, a five-hour jump on me!

Rex will be greatly disappointed in me and mad, and so will Captain Hilary, but I cannot blame them. I am disappointed in myself as well. He was in for a two-hour rebuke and lecture on staying alert, which I deserve! I, Borg have been outsmarted by a woman, not a good feeling! I am still in debt to Rex for a favor if he will still consider me reliable, which I doubt. Ha!

Borg went back to his car to go and tell Rex the bad news, but the car would not start. Raising the hood, the battery cables were corroded;

taking out his pocket knife he scraped them and reattached them to the battery, it started but he was empty of gas, just enough to get to a gas station, which turned out not to be his brand. Now Peggy has a six-hour jump on me, nice going!

When Borg did get to Rex's street, two moving vans was going down the street and when he got to Rex's house, there was no sign of anybody home at Peggy's house. Borg made an excuse to go over there; he was interested in the artist who painted his picture. Nobody was home.

Rex was home, so Borg went in and told him the bad news. Rex tensed up, told Borg he saw a van backed up next door and they loaded big plain boxes into the van, but he had no idea where Borg was or if he had been waylaid somewhere. Rex and Borg ran out to his car and started to follow the vans a distance ahead of him; but unfortunately, two traffic lights stopped him, while the vans were lost in traffic.

"See there. I told you, how does it feel to be outwitted by a woman? What made you think you could not be outsmarted by a woman any-way?" Rex asked with a smirk. I told you she was witty and smart! Now, she is gone, unless she is at the art gallery! If she isn't, you still owe me a favor, but it would be a total waste" Rex stormed away, tensed and testy, returning home and hearing this.

Rex and Borg raced over to the art gallery to see Kathy getting into her car. Rex hurried over toward her car but on seeing Rex she sped away, running a red light. However, Rex got her license plate number, the gallery locked up; Rex with Borg in the car drove straight to police headquarters to tell Captain Hilary.

"Are you bringing me good news or bad news? I don't need any bad news!"

Rex told him the bad news, and explained, on hearing about Borg, the captain laughed and shook his head.

"Borg is your backup, huh?" Hilary grimly inquired with a mocking smirk. "You are in bad shape if he is your backup (Hilary still laughing, Borg totally embarrassed). As for the face of Peggy, she probably already has changed her name and looks too, no news as to who she really is. As for her license. I will run it again to see who she really is, see what we come up with hopefully. We really have reason to check her out now."

Captain Hilary asked if they checked with the neighbors to see if they had seen or heard anything. Borg admitted they had not but "we will." The captain tensed and angry, lectured him sternly on staying alert.

"Rex, you check with the neighbors. I and my deputies will check the art gallery and place some plain-clothed deputies to watch the place. Borg, you go back to your regular job, whatever you were doing. We don't need you. I think and hope Rex has learned his lesson!" Borg is angry but keeps quiet, being embarrassed and humiliated from not only his own stupid mistakes but them laughing as well.

Rex described the Arabic-looking person. Borg told of his trip to Palo Alto Hotel and staying in the lobby to 1:00, then went to his room to listen for Peggy but fell asleep, that recliner was most relaxing. I awoke at 8:30 to rush downstairs to see if Peggy had checked out. She checked out at 4:00, by the time I got my car fixed, I need a newer one, and got gas; she had a six-hour jump on me, the first time I have been outsmarted by a woman. Hilary and Rex hearing that roared with laughter. Judy came in to see what was so funny, after they told her she was laughing too, Borg feeling foolish.

"She didn't go out at all, as to why she went there, I don't know. She used the name, Linda Guardable signing in," Borg said

"She might have taken care of business the next morning before you woke up or to throw you off if she was aware of you following her," Hilary stated. "I will check out her room and see if she made any phone calls or went out. Anything else?"

"No, that's it," Borg quietly replied, still embarrassed and humiliated by his stupid mistakes and them laughing, "I should have kept my mouth shut."

"Rex, you can look at some mug shots and see if the rough guy or the Arabic is one of them, hopefully, we'll get a break there and maybe at Palo Alto too. We need one now." A deputy gave Borg a ride back to his car.

After an hour Rex picked out the rough person's picture, a convict on parole convicted of assault with a deadly weapon, breaking and entering, and verbal abuse in public. Not a nice person, previously charged with an attempted murder but was acquitted due to a lack of evidence, his name, Luke Leprous, considered temperamental, and easy to provoke. Rex could not find the Arabic's mug shot if there was one.

Two detectives secretly posted within fifty yards of the art gallery on both sides and thirty yards of the parking lot. A deputy posted within thirty yards behind the art gallery as well. A deputy rented an empty office across the street. As for the rough person, two detectives went to his house to question him about his connection to Peggy Lausanne but he was not home. They questioned the neighbors and staked out his house to await his return. The neighbors said he stayed to himself and seldom went out, except to buy groceries, but never had any company.

"What do you want? I've been a good boy and not violate my parole."

"I'm Lieutenant Bruce Connors and my partner is Sergeant Harry Ballenger, we'd like you to come to headquarters for questioning in regard to Peggy Lausanne."

"Who is she? I don't know her, I've never heard of her."

"Maybe not by name, but we have a picture of you talking to her and you let her inside your house, she stayed for an hour and then left. You must have had something to talk about." Bruce produced a picture of Peggy and him and showing it to him, Luke disgusted but surprised.

"Ah, you recognize her, you are not to have any dealings whatsoever with any people of questionable or suspicious character and you know that, being on parole! That is a violation of your parole and you know that also!"

"I didn't know she was of 'questionable or suspicious' character as you say, am I under arrest for something I didn't know?"

"We don't know that, but you're coming with us for questioning, if you cooperate and answer our questions truthfully, we'll bring you back here. You should know who you are talking to before letting them in your house!"

At the police precinct, he was questioned for two hours before he began to talk, she wasn't Peggy Lausanne as they thought but Anne Towers, she is the one who embezzled the organization. He did not know much about her, he was the maintenance and errand man for the organization at the time. Anne had her own corner office. He never knew what was in the messages he was to deliver, he just delivered them, he said. He had to list whom he delivered messages for and to whom he delivered them.

Captain Hilary informed Rex that they are now investigating an extremist organization, thanks to you: however, the money is still a mystery as to where it is after leaving Peru National Bank. They are questioning the leaders and officials and may go before a grand jury, more than likely. No indictments yet but they will come. The grand jury will want to question you as well. I do not know about your involvement with "Miss Peggy" or "Anna Towers" but it will come out in the grand jury. I do not know about your partner either, Hilary laughing at that.

Rex smiled sheepishly and replied, "He was 'my ex-partner' and he owed me a favor for saving his butt in blowing an investigation."

Hilary said, "I understand that and I remember the investigation and Borg blowing it. The grand jury will want to know how you stumbled onto this 'Miss Peggy' among other things. You are in this now," Hilary declared,

"Yeah, that may put me in harm's way," Rex weary replied.

"If you feel you need protection or if it comes to that, you will be under protection twenty-four hours a day, day and night. That Luke Leprous is under surveillance, we could not hold him, nothing to connect him seriously other than Peggy Lausanne being in his house. He said he did not know about her being under suspicion, says her name is Anne Towers. The police are circulating flyers with Peggy's or Anne's picture around the post offices, banks, and government buildings in around and out of town, even to Palo Alto, using both of her names. Hilary wondered why she went to that hotel in that town. The FBI is tracking her background and financial records, and history under both names with banks, institutions, to charities and clubs. The flyers were hand delivered to real estates, proprietor associations and the police in Palo Alto. They need a break too."

Basics Real Estate at the edge of Palo Alto called their police who called Berkeley Police to report the real estate sold Peggy a house just outside of town in a small community five years ago. Berkeley Police asked if Peggy still lived there but the Palo Alto Police had no way of knowing, she had not committed any crime there, not even a ticket. They would check and see.

Detectives Bruce Connors and Harry Ballenger went to Palo Alto to accompany the police there to check out the house in the small community, with a search warrant in hand. The ranch type house new vacated, except the furniture is still there. There is the possibility she might return, the furniture still being here.

The neighbors on both sides said she had left with suit cases like she was going on vacation about two months ago, which was shortly after she had left the house in Berkeley. One neighbor mentioned that Peggy put a briefcase in the backseat: the neighbor figured she was going on a business trip of some sort. The neighbors could not understand why the police were interested in Peggy; she seemed like such a nice woman, always friendly and helpful; Peggy even helped in getting a woman's charity started.

After an official picked the door lock the detectives entered the house. By not damaging the lock or the door, maybe Peggy would not be able to tell the police had been there if she came back. Nothing there other than the furniture, in a backroom behind a desk, there was a set of plug-ins for computers, but no sign of the computers, disks or CBs. They could trace the computers if she used them. The detectives then went to the Palo Alto Hotel to look at the room Peggy had stayed in, Captain Hilary already there, but found nothing.

A call came in to Lieutenant Connors that a couple of business-like men had gone to the Luke Leprous house and he let them inside his house. The officers had taken down the license plate number and called it in to run it, do not harass them, or disclose your presence, but continue their surveillance. If the two leave follow them at a distance but do not lose them and do not let them SEE you! An hour later, the two men left heading for the expressway 24, going east, at expressway BBB, they turned north on BBD to expressway BD, after stopping off for gas, after a long drive, around one hundred and forty miles, to the Nevada State Line. The Nevada State Police contacted the FBI in Nevada, being the two had crossed the state line. The FBI called the state police back, to send two plain clothed officers to follow them from the state line and see where they go. Crossing into Nevada, the two stopped to get gas, stretch and have lunch, and then went south toward Carson City. The FBI took up the trail.

A trace was placed on the two businesspersons to identify them as to who they are and their line of work. The Palo Alto Police assigned two stakeout officers to stake out the house in the small community and Berkeley Police assigned two stakeout officers to watch Peggy's house next door to Rex. If Peggy or someone came back to either house, they might get a break by following and staking them out where they lived or were hiding.

One day a young girl pulled up in Peggy's driveway next door to Rex, went into the house for half hour, and came out. While she was inside, Officer Stuart Pullman called in her license number for a check, but she was clean far as any record with the police. They followed her out of town to a lower income community; Rex watched Peggy's house until another stakeout showed up; Peggy might show up, maybe but Rex doubted it. She is too smart for that.

Meanwhile, the hunt is on for the organization's income, their names and who they actually are in the organization, and what role do they actually play. There just might be a certain few-suspected congressional representatives with extremist ideas and a source of income and moral support, Maybe? There are certain corporations suspected as well. It would all come out in the grand jury inquiry; there will be at least some indictments handed out that is for sure! Their activities were being investigated which would be further looked into by the grand jury. The question is where the lead would go and how high up?

"You certainly opened a can of worms this time, Rex," Captain Hilary said smiling grimly.

"That wasn't my intention, maybe next time I'll just mind my own business and stick to the cases assigned to me," said Rex nervously, wondering why he stumbled into this.

"If you suspect a crime or something going down that doesn't seem right or looks suspicious you're supposed to report it, which you did. You are an officer of the court! You did the right thing reporting her, what you're supposed to do!"

"If I don't get hit," replied Rex.

"If you notice any suspicious activity around your house, your office, or someone following you, call me," Hilary said.

"You can count on that, I mostly work from my house than office; at my house, I'm home."

As Rex pulled away from the police precinct, a car half a block back, pulled out following Rex for a couple of miles, then turned off, to be picked up by another car pulling in behind Rex a block away and followed him to within six blocks of his house. As Rex was driving down the street in the middle lane to his street, an old truck eaten by rust, parked on the other, left-hand side of the street, going the other way. Suddenly it lurched across the street and straight at Rex at a high speed hitting him on the driver's side, slamming Rex's car back into the car behind him, and then speeding off. All that Rex saw was a man wearing black shades and a cap pulled low in an old truck coming straight at him but no time to react or move out of the way. Then everything went black. The car following Rex five cars back sped away as well, unnoticed, everyone looking at Rex.

Captain Hilary on hearing the report coming in of Rex Morgan being hit in a hit and run, rushed to the scene to get a report and check on Rex's condition. "Just don't let Rex die," Hilary kept muttering prayerfully. They were fitting Rex with a neck collar just as the captain pulled up. The Crime Scene Unit were there investigating and scanning the hit and run scene using a Crime Scene 3-0 Scanner, with the area closed off with crime scene yellow tape. They had to rip Rex's door off with the "Jaws of Life" to get to him, his head laid back and unconscious. Forensic had already taken pictures of Rex, his car and the crime scene, including the car behind him. Rex's car a total wreck, it was a miracle he was alive, judging from the impact.

Both ABC and NBC News were there in a few short minutes to cover the hit and run.

"What happened, did anyone actually see the accident and what happened?" asked Hilary stressed at seeing Rex.

"A woman in the third car back saw a man wearing black shades and a green cap pulled low in a rusted old pickup truck come speeding real fast from over there (pointing across the street) and drove straight into him. He drove this man back into the woman behind him, then sped off without bothering to stop," stated the Crime Scene Specialist. "The woman in the second car was knocked backward, giving her a severe neck whiplash. He has a severe neck whiplash also and a real nasty bump on the forehead, knocked unconscious and more than likely a serious concussion according to the Medical Examiner."

"The guy didn't intend to stop; this was a deliberate hit and run," retorted Captain Hilary. "Did you get the names, addresses and phone numbers?" Hilary asked, worried about Rex's condition.

"Yes sir, I did, I've put it in my report also," the specialist replied, handing the list to Hilary. Hilary said, "Good," looked at the list and put it in his pocket.

As they put Rex into the ambulance, Captain Hilary walked over to the woman who saw the hit and run, still a little shaky. "I'm Captain Hilary of the Berkeley Police Department. If you feel well enough: did you see the hit and run?"

"Yes sir, I did. I saw the whole thing. The guy in the truck came gunning at a high speed his engine from over there (pointing across the street) and slammed into that car up there in the side, driving him back into this woman in front of me," she replied (pointing to the car in front of her). "I thought at first she was going to be driven back into me."

"Do you think you could identify or describe him?"

"I didn't get a real good look at him but I think I could identify and describe him."

"Good, we need you to come to police headquarters and go over some pictures to see if you recognize him or describe him to our artist."

"Okay."

"Captain, this hit and run, did it have anything to do with the ongoing investigation of Peggy Lausanne and her involvement with the organization she worked for?" Jan Roberts from ABC News asked.

"We don't know what this accident involved. It just now happened. We can't say, we have to take everything into account."

"Captain, the truck came over there (pointing to across the street) at a high rate of speed straight deliberately and slammed into the guy in the car and took off, it looks like 'hit and run.'" Jan exclaimed. "Rex Morgan bringing to light about this Peggy Lausanne, it looks like she wanted to shut him up!"

"We don't know this, we're not prepared to say for now," Hilary replied uncomfortably. "It could be from one of his many other cases. He has made a lot of people look bad. Where are you getting your information?"

"Captain, this is part of my job to know and find out these things. Back to my question, it looks like she or somebody wants to shut Rex Morgan up. How could it possibly be anything else, what else could it be?" Jan asked with the ABC TV camera trained on Hilary.

"That is all I'm willing to say for now until this investigation is completed, we're not prepared to say for now. We don't know who that guy was."

"Ah, you know but you're not talking," Jan declared, seeing Hilary is nervous, knew she had "hit a home run with the bases loaded in the bottom of the ninth inning," Captain Hilary noticeably nervous knowing it would be in the news. Jan had hit a nerve.

"Just where did you get your information, just how do you know all of this?" Captain Hilary demanded.

"It's my job to know and I can't disclose my sources," Jan replied, sensing the captain's tension, time to back off.

At the hospital, Rex Morgan was under airtight security, no visitors without top security clearance, including the hospital staff on the ninth floor, trauma cases taking that floor. There were video cameras already in use on the floor and at each end of the hallway, at the nurse's station, the elevators and in the ceiling of the elevators, the lounge, family station and the lobby as well.

X-rays and tests run, the x-ray showing Rex had a serious concussion on the left side, close to the brain. He went into surgery immediately, a two and half hour operation plus cleaning up. Two officers posted outside his room around the clock and everything went in and came out be inspected by one of the officers. The surgeon said it would be a good number of days that Rex would be unavailable to talk. A suspicious looking person taken into custody was asking some questions at the main information desk in the lobby. As it turned out that, the organization hired him to find out if Rex Morgan had survived the accident but he knew nothing about the hit and run. The police let on like Rex had died during the operation. The press waiting outside the hospital informed by the hospital staff spokesperson that Rex had died due to complications of the concussion surgery on the left side of the brain. Hilary stated there would be no details until further in the investigation and no suspects had been taken into custody as of now.

"Sir. I understand there was a woman who saw the 'hit and run,' was she able to give a description of the suspect driver who got away?" asked Harold Jabots from NBC TV News Live. Jan Roberts from ABC News was close by listening and watching everything said, and reading expressions.

" She gave a vague description but she only got a glimpse of him as he passed by, he had his cap pulled low, not enough to go on and she didn't recognize anybody in any mug shots due to his cap pulled low," stated Captain Hilary, spotting Jan Roberts. Jan felt he was lying but proving it would be hard. "If anyone knows anything or hears anything, it would be appreciated if you would notify the authorities or if you see anything suspicious relating to this case."

"Captain Hilary, you're saying the woman wasn't close enough to be able to recognize or describe him?" Jan Roberts inquired, very suspicious. She is going to blow this investigation, Hilary though tensed.

"Yes, that is correct, he had his cap pulled low, he had on shades and she only got a side glimpse of him as he sped past her," Captain Hilary replied, nervously, which Jan noticed.

Truth is, the woman, Sheila Croswell, gave a fair description of the suspect, considering he was wearing black shades and a green cap pulled low, she only looked at his face and then the truck after he went by her, but didn't see any license plate. That information was to be secret from the press, and so the Militia would not know. Hilary felt Jan Roberts suspected him of lying. It is going to be difficult keeping information from her, Hilary felt, very difficult. I need to talk to her about that.

At police headquarters. Sheila looked through police mug shots on file and picked out a picture; she was positive it was he after an hour, Luke Leprous. A warrant issued for his arrest, Detectives Connors and

Ballenger drove to his house but his car was not in the driveway nor the truck, which they figured it would not be after the hit and run. They knocked at the door anyway but nobody answered, looking in the windows saw there no sign of anyone home. The detectives sat down the street waiting for him to come home, waiting all day and night, he never showed: they called in that he never came home; a search warrant was issued and delivered to them. With the search warrant in hand, they broke the door and entered to see what they could find. With the phone messages erased, there was nothing else there. Calling in that there had been nothing found and the phone messages erased, they were to bring the phone and message recorder in anyway, forensic might be able to track the messages anyway through recovery.

The next day a report came in that a body had been found under some bushes at the far end of a park across town but there is no identification on him. Detectives Connors and Ballenger drove there to discover it was Luke Leprous. Being that he had not come home last night, they were not surprised. The Medical Examiner, and ABC and NBC News were there with their camera crews to cover everything. Crime Scene Unit had the area closed off but the news camera crews could pick it up from behind the yellow tape. The Medical Examiner stated he had been dead about ninety hours, which would be why he didn't come home, he was already dead; Leprous failing his mission to kill Rex, if they knew or not, was no longer of any use and now expendable to keep him quiet. There was no reason for Leprous to make a hit on Rex on his own; it had to be someone had him to do it. The circumstance pointed back to the organization although it would be hard to prove. Leprous might have had enemies of his own, but he was a loose end that had to be expired. Peggy Lausanne could have just as well hired Leprous to hit Rex for exposing her. If she did, she must be around somewhere unless she used a messenger to negotiate an agreement but that would make her expendable as if she was not already a target, she would also be on the hot seat with the FBI. Who had more reason to hit Leprous if not the Militia organization? Peggy? It is possible but not likely. The "first officer" on the scene identified him as Luke Leprous: he had recognized him from earlier dealings with him.

"Was the victim in anyway tied to the ongoing investigation and Rex Morgan's hit and run?" Jan Roberts asked.

"We can't say right now, we don't know, it may be someone had something against him," Sergeant Ballenger replied.

"Come on, give us a straight answer for once! I understand he had a police record and was on probation, any comment on that?" Jan asked, suspicious of getting the "runaround" again.

"I can't comment on something like that, that would be violating his privacy and I'm not at liberty to say on such matters as that on a victim. To comment on a parolee's record is an ethical violation and I could be sued or go before the Ethics Board! You should know that!"

"Just trying to get some straight answers without getting the 'runaround.' They're still not talking: they have to check Captain Hilary first."

"Why the closed-mouth, the victim is dead," declared Harold Jabots from NBC News Live, becoming weary of getting the "runaround" as well.

"We don't know who he was involved with, if he was, or what he was involved in. We have to make sure, before we can say. We cannot be making statements without confirming them first! We cannot comment on a victim's record or violate his privacy! You should know that!"

Sergeant Ballenger received a call that Leprosy's car, a '50 Chevrolet Biscayne, found abandoned on a country road outside of Oakland, a total wreck. They must have towed it here after the wreck, Rex's picture found under the driver's seat. A sheriff's deputy had called it in to run a check on it; he had to get the number off the engine block. The detectives drove there to check it out and have it brought back to Berkeley.

Rex had recovered from the operation and was awake but with a terrible headache. The nurse gave a sedative putting him out again. He awoke after lunch the next day but still drowsy, hungry, but the nurse fed him despite him being drowsy. He was temporarily on a light diet. It was the doctor's order that he does not do much talking, answer any questions, or be disturbed but total rest for the next week, then maybe. The following week on the eighth day, the doctor told Captain Hilary to go very easy on him, very little questioning and nothing stressful. Hilary told Rex about Leprous being the one who hit him and being killed himself, and his car on a country road. Hilary suspected a possibility of Peggy behind Rex's hit and run but figured Rex would not accept that, and the doctor said nothing stressful.

The following week Hilary was back and Rex was feeling better, but still easy on the questioning and nothing stressful so Hilary expressed his suspicion of Peggy hiring Leprous to hit him. Rex right away said he did not believe she would do that

"I just don't believe she is the murderous type, unless it was for self-defense or she was cornered," Rex stated.

"Could it be that you feel that way because you're emotionally involved, maybe subconsciously?" Hilary asked with a smile.

"No she is a beautiful woman and it would be easy to fall in love with her but I'm not that easy. No, it is a gut feeling she is not the one. I am not saying she might not do it if pushed beyond the limit. I believe she could. However, anyone pushed beyond the limit will break eventually. I don't believe it was her, it was the organization."

"I believe you are right but we have to look at the possibility that it could be her. You sent her fleeing; she bought that house and had settled in, and then she had to drop everything and run," observed Hilary.

"Yeah, and that is the part I hate. I hold Borg responsible for that (Hilary laughing, agrees), but why did it have to be her to be mixed up in this? Why couldn't it be someone from a different neighborhood, like someone I don't know?"

"You're in an emotional web with her but don't get yourself worked up over this, you've got to get well," said Hilary smiling. "The doctor

said to take it easy on you for now, so I better wait until later on this."
Hilary leaving, Rex called the nurse for something to calm him.

"Did he get you worked up? I'm reporting to the nurse, the doctor said no stress!" The next ten days Rex just rested: go for a short walk in the hall, get checked by the doctor and eating light meals, Hilary dropping to check on him. The doctor said he is recovering well; go easy on him, not too much questioning, and nothing stressful yet! Hilary decides to wait another week to pick up where they left off, Hilary felt he had to know if Rex was hiding or protecting Peggy so she can be located and brought back as a material witness, before she disappears. The following week, the doctor said Rex is doing well and coming along good.

Hearing that, Hilary decided to pick up where they left off on the case of Rex and Peggy. "The grand jury is going to want to pick your brain and see what you know. They will be grilling you about your relationship with her; they might even suspect you of hiding her. For your sake, I hope you're not."

"Yes, I have no idea where she is. I know I'll be grilled by the grand jury, but I am not hiding her. Why couldn't it have been someone else, why was it her?"

"I can't help you: there are some things you'll have to work out. I have not seen her, she must be pretty (Hilary smiling) but she is wanted for questioning in these charges, remember that. Do not let your emotions carry you beyond that for now. Don't get in too deep just yet, until this is cleared up."

"Oh I know it would be a mistake to get emotionally involved right now, at least until this is cleared up. I understand that," admitted Rex.

"You might be right; it might be the organization, I feel you're right and I'll go on that assumption for now until I find something different and leading to her but don't expect me to 'put all my eggs in one basket' just yet. We'll get to the bottom of this, keep your chin up and I'll see you later."

"Just keep me informed of what's going on, if you hear anything from her. I'd like to talk to her."

"Okay, see you later." With Hilary leaving, Rex buzzed the nurse and requested something to calm his nerves.

In Palo Alto, there was a car seen driving slowly by Peggy's house, at the end of the street it turned around and came back, then drove away. A neighbor wrote down the license number and description of the car, a woman driving. The neighbor did not get a good look at the woman from the porch. The woman was looking at the house both coming and going down the street. A light green two-door hardtop older sedan, the license was from Las Vegas, Nevada, registered to Lana Coleman. There is nothing known about her other than she was a twenty-seven-year-old divorcee who worked at a local party store.

A surveillance team assigned to watch her to see where it would lead at her house and her job; all these leads should lead to somewhere eventually, just a matter of time, patience, and expense. As for the Militias Militia organization, nothing new had broken or turned up yet. They had gone to ground far as letting anything out, and well behaving themselves, everyone being shut-mouth, refusing to answer any questions without their attorney present. Laying low and wait for them to make a mistake, a game of cat and mouse. Peggy for sure had gone to ground if she was still alive.

While Rex was recovering in the hospital, two detectives were staying in Rex's house, watching Peggy's house. Two women came to the door claiming to be collecting money to help pay the hospitalization and medication of some little boy injured in an accident. The women engaged the detectives in conversation for a couple minutes, and then one asked if she could use the bathroom; she had to go. Reluctantly, Detective Nick Nelson let her in keeping the other woman at the door. Detective Larry Ottoman, at the window kept watch on the bathroom door while watching Peggy's house. The woman coming out of the bathroom tried engaging him in conversation.

"I noticed you keep looking out the window, what are watching or should I say who?"

"Why are you asking, Miss _____?"

"Just asking, I didn't mean to be nosey, just trying to make conversation."

"Are you through, we don't have time to answer a bunch of questions. Sorry."

"I could use a glass of water if it's not too much trouble, sorry to bother you, it looks to me like you have nothing but time, just sitting and looking out the window."

"The glasses are in the kitchen, we're rather busy right now."

"Could we be of help?"

"No, you can't help us, besides I thought you were collecting money for some boy in the hospital."

"We are, but we can take a break, but if you don't want us around, we can leave."

"I could use a drink too, it's been awhile since we had water," said the woman at the door. "Why is he being so rude?"

"We're very busy and don't have time to socialize, he's the nervous type and he's on medication. Sorry."

"It must be really secretive whatever you're working on."

"We can't say or disclose anything. Sorry."

The detectives followed the women to the kitchen wondering why they had come and what their real mission is for being here. Their fingerprints on the glasses might help to identify them if they are on file with the police, FBI or the Interpol. "Do you women live around here?" Ottoman asked.

"A couple blocks away, why do you ask?" the one woman asked, suspiciously.

"Just wondering why you came here to this house. I haven't seen you going to the other houses. I thought maybe we could get together sometime for dinner."

"No thanks, you two are weird and secretive or something." With that said, they left as if in a hurry.

"Strange them coming here, I wonder if they really were collecting money for some child or just trying to distract us?" pondered Connors.

"I wander too." Ottoman calls Captain Hilary to report the visit of the two women, hearing the report the captain thought it strange and suspicious too. "Could be they wanted to check and see if Rex was home," Hilary stated.

"Yeah, that's what we were wondering, or if it could be they wanted to distract us while someone slipped back into Peggy's house next door. The one woman said they live a couple blocks over."

"She probably was lying; did they pull you away from the window?" Hilary asked, already suspecting the answer.

"For two or three minutes, the one wanted to use the bathroom, and then she wanted a drink, then the other one wanted a drink as well. They left their fingerprints on the glasses," stated Ottoman.

"What could they possibly have wanted, there is nothing over there but the furniture." There must be something hidden there that we missed, there must be."

"Maybe, but I don't see how, that place was searched room by room, and the basement too."

"Maybe you didn't look in the right places, hidden places; there has to be a reason for those women to distract you, did they look around, the woman using the bathroom, did she nose around any at all?"

"She glanced down the hall but other than that, no: we could be overlooking something, maybe, but I don't see how."

"If there is anybody there, question them as to why they're there and bring them in," commanded Captain Hilary; looking in Peggy's windows, there did not appear to be anybody there. Unlocking the door, the detectives went inside and looked around, checking each room and closet, looking for hidden doors and closets, even the basement as well, but finding nothing.

"Apparently, they just wanted to know if Rex was home, we better get back over there and call the Captain," returning to Rex's house they call the Captain, "Nobody over there, we checked room by room, even the closets and the basement too."

"They just wanted to know if Rex was home then, that had to be it, there's no report of any boy injured and hospitalized or even treated, someone is concerned if Rex is alive and well or not," commented Hilary cheerfully. "We've got them worried."

"Let's keep it that way," replied Ottoman hopefully. "If they keep worrying and snooping, maybe they'll make a bad mistake sooner or later."

"Exactly," agreed Hilary. The trouble is if they find out he is alive, they will be combing the hospitals until they find him. Hilary worried. I've got to get him out of the hospital as soon as possible if that's soon enough but where to? I cannot let anyone know except on a need-to-know basis. Everyone will have to be screened, especially those over his care! They are trying to locate and hit him before he goes to the grand jury. He says he only knows about Peggy, if that is her name. Luke Leprous said her name is Anne Towers. Apparently, the organization thinks Rex knows a lot more.

"Did you see where the women came from and where they went?" Hilary asked already suspecting the answer.

"No, I just saw them walking up to the door," Nick Nelson admitted, sensing Hilary's tension.

"You mean they almost got to the door before you saw them?"

"Yes, I was watching the news; it gets pretty boring just looking out the windows with nothing happening. I did not expect to see anyone coming to the door."

"Did you see where they went after they left or did you go back to watching the news?" Hilary retorted disgusted.

They walked down the street and turned the corner," replied Nick, ignoring the slur.

"You didn't follow after them to see where they went or what kind of car they had and get a license number?"

"No, I didn't think of that but maybe the neighbors saw their car if they had one."

"What did you think of, no, don't answer that!" Hilary mouthed off and slammed the phone down. No wonder we cannot find Peggy Lausanne, or Anne Towers or whatever her real name is. With this kind of help, we may not ever find her. Wait until Rex hears this. Hilary chuckled and shook his head. Whoever those women were, we will probably never know or whom they are working for: but one thing is certain, whoever sent them knows by now that Rex is not at home and Peggy's house is under surveillance now. It is doubtful that they will ever come there. They might go to Palo Alto if the police there do not give themselves away. Where do we go from here? Hilary felt a stressful heartburn coming on.

Checking with the neighbors down the street from Rex's house only one neighbor had noticed a car just sitting there at the corner, she didn't think anything of it. She didn't see any reason to be suspicious about the women or the car.

Berkeley State Bank called the County Bureau of Births and Deaths to inquire if Luke Leprous had died, a man, and woman had come in, inquiring if Leprous had a safety deposit box there. Their behavior and line of questioning were suspicious, they were there to pick up whatever he had. The bureau knowing he was under investigation, called Captain Hilary. The couple's proof of relationship was questionable also. Hilary called the bank to find out more about them and any new information on them.

"Have they left'?" Hilary inquired.

"Yes, they left saying they would be back, they could not understand how their documental proof of relationship could be out of order."

"Did you get their name and address?"

"Yes. I told them I would have to verify their relationship being that he did not list any relatives on his application. They said they would like to check with their attorney to make sure the documental proof was in order and their relationship being that Luke did not list them as relatives. I told them I could verify whether they were relatives or not but they wanted to consult with an attorney to see what they should do. They became suspicious when I continued to stall them with questioning their relationship: they were ready to leave. We have them on video at my desk."

"Good, sounds like a possible fraud, don't release that safety deposit box to anybody just now: the FBI will want to have a look to see what is in there. Do you remember where they were from?"

"Chicago, Illinois, their documents said." "Do you remember their address?"

"They said Vernon Avenue but I don't remember the house number."

"That is okay, the FBI will be able to trace it with this, if it exists. Contact the FBI; they can check this out. The FBI will want to check that out and see if they really are relatives. I will get back with you if I find out anything. You need to contact the FBI on this. Did they give you their names?"

"Mike and Joyce Leprous, they claimed to be uncle and aunt, they said his parents are dead."

With that said, Captain Hilary called the Chicago Bureau of Births and Deaths to see if there is a Mike and Joyce Leprous living there in Chicago. Yes, there is—a middle-aged couple; Mike should be forty-eight and Joyce should be forty-two. At least, that much is true but there is no record of a relative named Luke Leprous, same last name but no relationship? It is possible; could it be Luke Leprous's name is a fake? It is possible, but what if it is not a fake? What are they to Luke Leprous and just how did they know about him? Rex Morgan, this mystery is getting bigger and deeper with no answers, and you are laid up as well as a target. What is next? wondered Hilary, check with the FBI, I guess. Rex Morgan, do not die on me now, I need you alive.

Checking with the FBI, they were unaware that Luke Leprous had a safety deposit box, much less anyone trying to get to it. As for the

Leprous couple, they would check on them as to who they really are and what connection they had to Luke Leprous if any. As for him not having relatives, they had thought they were deceased. But they would take another closer look at him. The FBI contacted the Berkeley State Bank for a fax print of the couple Mike and Joyce Leprous so they could compare their picture to any mug shots on file if there were any.

Taking a closer look at Luke Leprous the FBI started comparing his picture taken by Rex Morgan to the mug shots on file but found nothing other than the one the police had. Calling for a Forensic Facial Profiler, Gary Bollinger, he started the comparison of the bone structure, facial and characteristic features to faces in mug shots in FBI files. After a full day of study and comparing faces and bone structures, he came up with an excellent match. Luke Leprous was the exact match of Max Guinean on five points and the facial features were similar but it looked like some changes had been made, giving him a new face. The cheekbones were similar, the chin, around the eyes, a high forehead and curve of the head.

Max Guinean wanted for the murder of the Attorney General, Anthony Gilmore, hot on the investigation of a gunrunning and smuggling operation fifteen years ago; and starting to get leads, the leads died with him. Gunned down with his chauffer in heavy traffic, the briefcase he had with him with the papers, notes, and disks taken. His office broken into, the material in his office deleted, the computer files and programs destroyed. his file cabinet rifled through. and the disk file on the desk empty. His home office had been broken into, the house ransacked and his material on the computer deleted, programs destroyed, file box empty and his file cabinet rifled through, while he was at the Capital while his wife, Pamela, was out shopping. The neighbor said she noticed a white van with a rack on top and a ladder on the side in the driveway, she figured an appliance repair truck. She did not see the technician and there was no name on the side of the truck.

The FBI checked with Interpol to see if they had anything on Max Guinean and he in connection to the gunrunning and smuggling, Interpol said they would check. They called back to say they tried to run a check on him, but they kept running into dead ends, they never were able to get anything on him. There was either nothing to get or he was high up enough that he was under protection. He had been in the same hotels, cafes and a number of bookstores on a number of occasions as had the leaders of gunrunning and smuggling operations. A one-time only meeting place or was it a regular arrangement? Who was protecting him and if so, why? Checking with the CIA his file was sealed and classified, he had done some work for the CIA was all they would say.

Max Guinean was the prime suspect for the murder being that he had been hanging around the Capital and Anthony Gilmore's neighborhood. However, as for who destroyed the computer and programs?—that remained a mystery. Max Guinean dropped out of sight after that, he up and disappeared after that. Now, who killed him and why? Had he become sloppy and useless in failing his mission to eliminate Rex Morgan, no longer skillful? Max could have cleared up a whole lot of questions; maybe that is why they eliminated him? As for Mike and Joyce Leprous, they are suspected of either being members or associated with the extremist organization, Malitias Militia in some way or another. They had not returned to their home in Chicago after three days; they apparently had gone to ground like all the others.

"We get one or two things cleared up and it opens up something else," Hilary told Rex.

"Well, that's better than nothing being opened up," Rex replied. "Did you ever find out anything on that Arabic looking person'?"

"No, nothing has come to light on him. I checked with the FBI and the CIA and they checked with Interpol. There was nothing. I guess eventually someday all of this will clear up if we keep opening doors, if they don't skip the country."

"Have fun," Rex smiled teasingly.

"Oh you are in it too, you just brought it to the surface, but you are in it with us," Hilary countered, smirking.

"But this has advanced beyond my line of work, even though I have learned some things from it."

"Yes, but you are not going to cut loose and walk away, you know too much. Besides, you are a target, are you sure you want to be cut loose?" asked Hilary mockingly.

"You are putting the squeeze on me now. Borg could help you," Rex said, smiling.

"That is real funny, ha-ha. He is your friend, not ours. We have our own flunkies, a couple of detectives staying in your house to watch Peggy's house let two women get almost to the front door before seeing them and gave away that they were there for a reason they couldn't talk about. Then they let the women get away without getting their names, where they live, and their license plate number. A woman down the street at the corner noticed a light blue older car at the corner but thought nothing of it, and she did not know what kind of car it was. I sent another detective asking the neighbors around there but nobody saw anything except the one neighbor."

"They are detectives and they messed up like that? Borg could have done that good or better," Rex stated, laughing and shaking his head.

"Yeah, I know," Hilary admitted bitterly; "don't mention him to me though, if it had not been for him, we might still have Peggy."

"Did you ever see where his Master Card charge went made out to the art gallery? That was his idea."

"Hey, that is right, I will have to check on that, thanks for bringing that to my attention; that is just one good deed he did, but he sure gave himself away to Peggy or Anne. We have not been able to locate her, she has gone to ground."

"Oh, she is a sharp one all right, too sharp for Borg and she has given me the slip too," Rex confessed. "Locating her will not be an easy task. I feel eventually we will find her, as for dead or alive, I do not know. That depends on whether you all find her first or the Militia. I would hate to be her if they find her first, and it would not be pretty."

"I am of the same opinion," said Hilary thoughtly.

"Who knows, she might give herself up to avoid being hit by the Militia if she sees them first, closing in."

"If she has the time, that would be a very wise decision on her part, it would help us in our investigation, and it would go easier on her with the court. She could open many doors and probably finger a number of people. She is on the FBI's Most Wanted list," stated Hilary.

"That is why the organization would like her dead: there would be a lot of red faces, probably including some government officials and maybe some congress representatives. Who knows where she could lead us. Someday, she could be caught speeding or a broken tail light or some little something, although I think she is more careful than that. Who knows, anything could happen."

"Or be found dead in some house or some park, or a field."

"Oh don't say that, I hope not," moaned Rex.

"Did you fall in love with her, all of these emotions, you are not hiding her are you?" quizzed Hilary.

"No, I am not hiding her, I have told you that already. You know me better than that," said Rex laughing. "She is sweet, kind, and down-right pretty, but I am not hiding her."

"Some pretty strong emotions there, were you intimate with her?"

"Captain. I am not going to answer that question, that is personal and has nothing to do with her disappearance or the investigation," replied Rex, stunned and a bit angry.

"You just answered my question and it could have a lot to do with the investigation if you are hiding her even though I do not think you would do that. You are not stupid, you know the consequences of that, but I had to ask after you expressing your strong emotions with her up and disappearing. The grand jury will question you intensely about your relationship with her; I figure you know that. You do not lie to the grand jury and I think you know that."

"Yes, I know that they will question me intensely about her and our relationship. I was not the cause of her disappearance, it Borg's fault entirely and our relationship did not have time to get going and did not affect my better judgment! I am not going to risk my career that I worked hard for so long over her, even though she is beautiful! Remember that I came to you about her where I could have waited or tend to the cases assigned to me, don't forget that!" Rex snapped.

"Okay, okay. Don't get so upset. I am just looking for some answers and possibilities same as the grand jury will be doing. You know that. I have to ask you these questions and 1 am preparing you for the grand jury grilling you will be getting by questioning you like this. They will grill you like I just did if not a lot more."

"Yes, I know they will grill me but you know me better than that, you know that I would not hide her, interfere with the investigation, or hold back any information if I knew anything! You know that! I would not risk my career for that!"

"I have to ask you anyway, that way I can say I have questioned you and be in the clear. That is my job, regardless of friendships, you know that, and I know you. Sometimes you do not always give the whole story and you are not above questioning no more than anyone else is! In an investigation, nobody gets off questioning. Friendships stops under the law. There are no favorites!"

"You are right, you are doing your job, even if it gives me a migraine headache, and I will be asked the same darn boring and insulting questions at the grand jury! But my emotions did not affect my judgment, do you want that in writing and me signing it?"

"Okay, good, that is cleared." Hilary feeling it is time to back off until Rex has recovered more, and he is already upset.

"If the computer forensics was to trace Peggy's computers they might be able to pull up something. What about that?" Rex asked, trying to calm down.

"They have tried to trace her computers that were at her house and the art gallery but we are at a blank. The computers and everything else at the house are gone but the computers at the art gallery we are not sure, any other ideas? We need a break."

"I have no more ideas for now, but I need something for the migraine and stress," Rex buzzing the nurse.

"Did he bring on this migraine and stress?" the nurse, pointing to Hilary.

"I had to get some straight answers from him," Hilary cut in, in self-defense. "I am sorry about that, but I have to do my job."

"Explain that to the doctor." replied the nurse. "He is here to recover, then go home. Though you can question him."

"Sorry."

Back at the precinct, a report came in for Captain Hilary on the bullet that killed Max Guinean, known as Luke Leprous. The bullet was a .44 magnum, probably a Smith and Wesson, shot from one hundred feet. Forensics declared it as a professional hit.

"Well, that would do the job, they meant for him not to survive. That is certain. Too bad we couldn't have got to him first, he could have opened a lot of doors, but that is why he was killed. I guess," stated Hilary. "Where do we go from here?" he pondered aloud worried what was next as he entered his office. Rex? I hope not, I need him even though I would never admit it openly to him. Hilary told Judy nothing concerning Rex in case someone tried to get answers from her.

At the hospital, a middle-aged looking man. disguised as a doctor to see Rex, taken into custody for questioning, trying to get into Rex's room. The officers on duty at the door became suspicious when he was not wearing the proper badge on his white coat and could not produce it. They did not recognize his name as a staff doctor as well. He had an identity badge as a doctor but it was not the right badge. As it turned out, he was not on the hospital staff, and none of the staff knew him, Herman Kopf, on his identity badge; he was questioned and his identity checked to see if he was really a doctor or not and why he came to Mercy General Hospital and to that room. His identity as a doctor checked out, he was a doctor on the staff of St. John Vicuna Hospital.

He claimed he received a call from this hospital, asking him to come to this hospital and check on Rex Morgan's recovery. They wanted an outside opinion from a doctor from another hospital, for confirmation of Rex's condition. A head staff doctor from this hospital called him, he said, the call was on his Caller ID at home, but the caller did not identify himself, just said he was the head staff doctor. He sounded like a real professional doctor. The head staff doctor, Joseph Knight, M.D. denied calling anyone by that name: he was in a staff meeting at one o'clock, shortly was confirmed. Kopf's Caller ID confirmed being called from this hospital, an inside service phone with hospital intercom in the background. A comparison of the voice on the Caller ID compared with Dr. Knight has showed it was not him. Captain Hilary on hearing the report, called the FBI about the security problem and Rex now has to move soon as possible!

"It is getting more difficult keeping his whereabouts a secret, whoever sent that doctor now knows where Rex is and that he is alive! I believe now more than ever that the Militia organization is behind this, so we have to move Rex. We will have to have a handpicked, top security clearance crew guarding him day and night!" Hilary stated under heavy stress.

"Yes. I agree, how did they find out where he was, the story was supposed to be that he died during the operation when he came in. Evidently, we did not screen the hospital staff for that floor good enough or maybe it could be that someone on one of the other floors? That would take a lot of time to screen the entire hospital staff! However, when word gets out that someone on a certain floor is getting special treatment, word can travel fast! Someone could have made the call from there without ever leaving and continue on with their job or it could be a jealous patient," replied the Regional FBI Director, John Cotter.

"Yes. I understand that but in light of what has happened, we have to move him now, soon as possible! We have to have top security clearance watching him, the Militia has shown it will do anything and stop at nothing to get to Rex so he will never reach the grand jury," stated Hilary, concerned where the leak is. This is going to give me an ulcer by the time we get Rex moved and already I have a migraine, Hilary thought wearily.

"Does Rex know anything on the organization, anything really damaging or just this 'Miss Peggy?' It seems like they are going to a lot of trouble to shut him down, does he know anything at all about their activities, their officials, or who their sources are?"

"Far as I can tell, he only knows about Peggy and I believe he has leveled with me on what he knows, I questioned and grilled him good if he knew anything at all and he said no. He knows I do not like being held back. He knows how I feel about that," assured Hilary.

"Maybe someone from here should have a talk with him, just to see if he knows anything damaging. Maybe he is not aware of what he does know or overlooked, or discarded?"

"You can give it a try after he has had more time to rest but I do not think he is ready for any more intense grilling than what I gave him right now; I don't think you will get any more than what he told me, I would be surprised if you did. Whomever you send will go through my clearance, and have to have my clearance, and I am firm on that! You can believe that!"

"Do you really think I have anyone within the FBI that would be associated with that organization? If there is any moles and I find out about it, they will go on trial in federal court as well lose their pension and service time, that would be the end of their career in law and the government: federal, state and local! That is a clear understanding within the FBI; we make sure that they are aware of that from the very beginning! In addition a federal trial is not as easy-going as state or a local trial! Upon conviction, they serve the full sentence, there is no parole under a federal conviction!" John retorted. "Let me know when we can question him to see if he knows anything at all. We need to question him!"

"No, I do not think there are any moles in the FBI but I do not want to find out that I was wrong. The check stands, they will go my clearance check, before they see Rex, much less, talk to him, and my men will be there with him the entire time! That is firm!"

"Okay, okay, have it your way on that but we get to question him! You cannot override that and you know that!"

"Okay, you question him after he recovers but the clearance is going to be my way or else it will not happen!" retorted Captain Hilary, angrily. "I can and I will insist on that; there have been too many close calls to relax now!"

At the hospital, the head doctor said Rex was able to move as long as he does not do anything heroic or labor but just rest and take it easy for at least a month and he comes back for a checkup every two weeks. He must take it easy, and totally relax and rest! That is an absolute must! On hearing that after the doctor had signed the release form with the conditions been clearly laid out, he had gone, Rex wanted to go back to Peggy's house to look around to see if anything had been overlooked and left behind.

"Are you crazy? Did you not hear the doctor just now say not to do anything but totally relax, rest and take it easy for a month at least? Besides, you are a target; someone wants you dead! D-E-A-D! Are you sure, you have told me everything you know? You have not kept anything back, like something on those computers. Someone wants you dead really bad, they have gone to a lot of trouble to hit you and the FBI thinks you know something you are holding back or do not realize you know," grilled Hilary. "What is it, Rex Morgan? Tell me!"

"There is absolutely nothing that I can think of! I have told you everything I know and can think of! How many times do I have to tell you that?" stormed Rex. "Those computers were too complex, a new type of code or something! I could not bring anything up, everything was locked down; as I have told you before or do you not remember that? Am I going to have to go through this again?"

"Well, someone does not believe that, and the FBI and I wonder why!"

"How am I supposed to know? I do not know why, maybe they think I know more than I actually do, maybe I saw something and I do not realize it! But I would like to explore that idea and find out, so you will get off my back!" yelled Rex.

"Maybe you are right, think back and if something comes to mind, spill it, even if it does not seem important. It may not seem important to you but to someone else, it may be very important. We have to explore every avenue of thought, even things that do not seem like much," lectured Hilary. "Are you sure you did not overhear or see something that could be damaging to the Militia, even if it does not seem important to you? Try to think, man, think!"

"I have been thinking, if I could remember anything I would tell you to get you off my back, I am tired of this! The man at the art gallery looked like someone from a Mid-Eastern or third world country, he might be someone I was not supposed to see, he turned his back quickly but I had already seen his face. He might have changed his looks to some degree from a mug shot or he might be someone that is supposed to be dead. I would recognize him if I see him again. Maybe that is why they are after me? Maybe I saw something in the backroom and I do not remember it? I did see some paintings back there that looked like they were ready to be shipped and some that looked like they were to go on display," Rex stated. "Some of the paintings were worth more than my annual income, way out of my budget! Kathy told me the 'Masters' painted them."

"That could be it, maybe you weren't supposed to see those, they might be stolen heirloom paintings but someone sure wants to make sure you do not remember or talk. That Mid-Eastern person, you think Peggy is associated with him, in some way or another?"

"That is hard for me to believe, she looked full-blood American and no foreign accent, if that means anything. It looked to me like they were in an intense argument, and she said he kept wanting her to lower her prices. However, there were no paintings around where they were arguing in that area of the room. But I don't believe she was associated with him in any way."

"She has got you wooed under her spell, she can be all-American and still be associated with him, they might have been arguing over little something or some technical problem, him wanting her to lower her prices sounds fishy."

"The way they were arguing I do not think it was anything minor, they were too angry, too intense; it looked like a very serious argument to me," Rex replied with Hilary smiling slightly. "I am in control of my emotions and I am thinking!"

"You might have something on the paintings, stolen heirlooms being smuggled through her art gallery; it would be a perfect setup in moving them. Let us get a sketch of the Arabic-looking man faxed to the FBI and Interpol: you think he might have changed his face? It is very possible he could have," replied Hilary in a better spirit now and sensing Rex is angry about the continuous grilling. "I will check with the FBI and Interpol on the paintings. I still feel you are not aware that you are under her spell, even though I have never met her."

"Captain, I am in control of my emotions and I am not under her spell and I do not believe she is associated with the Arab! I am, however, getting tired of hearing this! You keep this up, and we will part company and I will take my chances on my own," stormed Rex.

"You are far beyond feeling far as she doing any wrong, and I actually believe that, but I will back off," replied Hilary realizing Rex has had enough.

"You are enjoying this but you are dead wrong! You are dead wrong!"

"Why not. I have not had a good laugh in a long time; since this started, except when Borg lipped off about not being outsmarted by a woman. A good laugh once in a while relieves tension."

"Well, do not keep pushing it or we will part company!" declared Rex. "Let us go to Peggy's house and look in the unusual places, maybe your flunkies overlooked something unconsciously and not aware of it," said Rex trying to change the subject and cool down, "see if they missed anything." Hilary realizes Rex is real angry and tired of the continuous probing and teasing.

"Let us drop this tiresome taunting subject and get back to going to look her house over, top to bottom," said Rex still angry.

"Boy, you like punishment, okay just look do not lift or do any bending. If you get tired, we quit. Okay. First, we get that mid-eastern person's face over to forensics and see if he has had any changes, if he hasn't, we fax it to the FBI and Interpol. We will need a search warrant to protect ourselves from an 'unlawful search'."

"Okay. But this is no worse than the grilling, taunting, and boredom teasing. But it is much more stressful! I have had enough!" replied Rex still very angry and Hilary noticing it.

Pulling into Peggy's driveway, the detectives came running from Rex's house ready to starting to question Hilary and Rex.

"If we were hit men you two would be dead, charging across the yard like that," Hilary lectured them.

"Sorry sir, but we have been bored to death, nothing happening. There has been no activity whatsoever. We wait until dark to change shifts," stated Nick Nelson, trying to excuse himself and his partner.

"If they were down the street watching, they could still see you changing shifts, even in the dark" Rex commented. "That is probably why you have not seen activity."

"Yeah, I suppose so. Whatever," Nick replied, seeing it was useless making excuses.

"Oh well, you two detectives have done gave yourselves away that you're watching this house anyway." Hilary pointed out.

"Are you two here to remind us of our mistakes and rub it in?" Ottoman asked, weary of continuing being reminded of their past mistakes.

"No, but if we were, would it do any good?" asked Hilary with a smirk.

"Thanks, thanks a lot, go ahead, and rub it in good. Oh, by the way, forensics was here to see if anything was left far as the computers or anything else, we called to confirm they were from the forensics' lab."

"Good, I am glad you didn't take their word for it, I hope they showed their badges," stated Hilary.

"We are here to give Peggy's house a search from top to bottom," stated Rex, cutting in and tired of hearing Hilary.

"We have already did that," protested Nick, feeling stressed at always taking a slam. "That is why we are going over it again," stated Hilary.

"Well, go ahead but you will not find anything, I grant you that," retorted Ottoman, totally disgusted. "Go ahead, knock yourselves out!"

"We will see," countered Hilary. With that, the detectives storm back to Rex's house in total disgust. Inside Peggy's house, Hilary asked where do we start and Rex replied, "Look anywhere most unlikely to hide anything, the least likely or littlest thing could be vital to breaking open the investigation."

Hilary and Rex looked for an hour but came up empty; Rex suggesting they check out the basement, Hilary said we might as well. Down under, the bottom step was a small package wrapped in burlap, neatly tucked under the last step, almost impossible to see. On seeing it, Rex reached down and grabbed it.

"Ah, I found something, you walking in front of me, you missed it."

"What did you find?" Hilary asked, rushing over to see what he missed, excited.

"Something wrapped in burlap to protect it from the moist and basement elements." Opening it, Rex looked at a list of names and addresses. "You will want to check this out for sure, a list of names and addresses," Rex handing it to Hilary.

"Alright, finally at last, the break we need!" replied Hilary, excited. "See who all is on here, anyone we know," Hilary nervous with excitement.

Hilary and Rex continued to look around the basement, behind the snack bar on the floor, almost completely concealed under the bottom shelve was a book of matches. Rex reached down and pulled the matches out, "A book of matches with nothing on it but the manufacture of the matches."

"Hey, you are supposed to resting and relaxing," Hilary said laughing.

"Well, I can put them back and go rest and relax; give me that list and I will put it back, then go rest and relax." Rex teased, knowing Hilary would baulk at that.

"Ha-ha. Not now, being you found these, you're not putting them back: I will have these checked out, a fantastic find! You are better than both of my detectives which is not surprising."

"Well, thank you, should I stop and go rest?" asked Rex grinning, knowing the answer to that.

"Are you tired or feeling weak?"

"Not yet, but I wonder if this bar was raised, what would be underneath, if anything."

"You just wait and I will try to tilt it and you look and see." With Hilary tilting it, Rex looks underneath, but there was nothing there.

"Let us keep looking until we have covered everything, which I behave we have done," Hilary said anxiously; they continued looking in the rooms, checking the beverage bar and shelves on the walls but finding nothing, they went back upstairs to look one more time before leaving.

"We find out where the manufacturer distributed these matches, we can go there to see if they recognize Peggy or Kathy, and how they came by these matches," stated Hilary happily.

"It could be just someone just visiting here, although I never saw anyone coming here. How about the window shades? Sometimes people hide money or something in them and roll them back up," stated Rex.

"Okay, I will get them down though," Hilary standing on his toes and reaching up, took down the window shades. Completely unrolling the shades but there was nothing.

"Well, that is it I guess, it wasn't a wasted trip," breathed Hilary happily, as they go over to Rex's house. Hilary waves the burlap package and book of matches as they enter the house.

"You found that over there? I do not believe it!" Ottoman stammers, shocked. "Where did you find it?"

"Rex found this burlap package under the last basement step and this book of matches under the bottom shelves of the snack bar in the basement. Now, you see why we went back over there. I wonder what else you have overlooked?" stated Hilary.

"Thanks, thanks a lot, did you come here to rub it in, our mistakes in not noticing the women, not getting their license number, and now miss seeing those? If you did, being that Rex is here, we are leaving," Ottoman declared.

"Isn't that enough mistakes?" asked Hilary.

Nick Nelson sitting on the couch watching and listening, spoke up, "It would be a relief if you would send us someone to give us a break or to talk to once in a while, it gets really boring just sitting here looking at that house over there and nothing happening."

"You are supposed to watch the street also, to see if someone drives or walks by," retorted Hilary: "That is how stakeouts usually are."

"We kept a watch on the street, except that one time, an occasional neighbor walked by, but that is all," replied Nick.

"Well, I am home now, so you guys can take off now, anyway, if that is okay with your captain?" stated Rex, trying to ease the friction.

"It is okay I guess. But if you see anything, call me," stated Hilary to Rex. "There will be a patrol coming around to keep watch in case anybody comes nosing around."

"If they did, by the time police got here, the culprits could be done and gone." commended Rex.

"You are probably right, but there's always the chance that they will get caught," admitted Hilary. With that said, the two detectives figuring that was enough insults, left.

"By the way, Peggy said her parents live in West Virginia, and a sister lives at home and is going to college, majoring in landscape design. I do not think Peggy would go back there and endanger her parents and sister; and with the law and the organization after her. However, her parents and sister might know something or know where she is or where she is staying. I would like to just sort of 'drop in' to visit them to see if they do know something, where she is? Or where she is staying? I might be able to come up with something there, they may not know what she's done or is involved in," stated Rex.

"You might have something there but we need to question them about Peggy and see if they know anything," put in Hilary.

"Detectives or agents showing up at the parents' home more than likely would put Peggy on the run for sure, if they do know where she is. I could ask them in around about way without upsetting them; I think I could tell if they know anything helpful to the investigation. I have learned to tell if someone knows more than they are telling," Rex stated.

"You really think you could? If they do know something more than they are telling or willing to tell, you are sure you could tell if they are withholding something?" quizzed Hilary.

"That was my job in the service to quiz and question prisoners and suspicious people. If they do know something and they are not willing to talk, then the law could step in; first give me a chance. However, the way

Peggy talked about her parents and sister, I do not see her involving them in this and putting them at risk. She loves her parents and respects them; she loves her sister too. Nevertheless, they may just know something of what she does; but not know her involvement in all of this. Why burden them with this if we don't have to and they do not know about this?" pleaded Rex. "Why bully them when we don't need to?"

"True, you are right, but if they know anything but will not talk, then we have to question them," stated Hilary. "Good thinking, excellent idea. First, you have to recover your health, get a checkup from the doctor, and we would want a full report. However, if the FBI finds out about this, I cannot hold them back. I can talk to him, but I cannot hold him back if he decides to question them. The FBI could hold a possible material witness from us under circumstances, but I cannot hold them back."

"Oh, I know that. I was in the FBI once, I would wait until I completely recover before going there, but if you talk or tell them anything before I have had a chance to recover and talk to Peggy's parents, the FBI will go ahead and not wait to question them. After interviewing and talking to them, I would send a full report or deliver it personally. If the FBI bullies their authority in questioning them, it will ruin everything, and I will not forget that! I promise you that."

"Yeah. I know you will, I believe you but I promise if the FBI bullies their authority, I will flat forget it, I promise you"

"Oh, I believe you but you might be better to fax it in case someone tries to make a hit on you again," Hilary recommended.

"True, you're right, is the FBI ever going to get a search warrant for that organization or wait until they have destroyed everything if not already? Is someone deliberately delaying the process to give them more time to destroy everything?"

"That is up to the FBI, I cannot do anything about that, the organization headquarters is in another state. If they were in this state. I could move on them being they are within my jurisdiction but the headquarters is in another state. As to why the FBI and the Justice Department hasn't moved on them I do not know, maybe the organization has or knows someone in high places of authority, which wouldn't be a surprise to me."

"I suspect they know somebody up there, maybe even have them on a 'string': they have something on somebody up there or someone is working for them for favors, I am sure of that," stated Rex tensed.

"I feel the same way," added Hillary. "Borg's Visa charge was traced to Berkeley State Bank, here in Berkeley, but the account was closed shortly thereafter, no surprise to me."

"Naturally. Peggy would not leave anything open like that; she is too smart for that. All the accounts were probably places here in Berkeley."

"Yes, how did you know?" asked Hilary, surprised.

"I just know her. Her way of doing business, hard to get anything on her; you and the FBI will find that out if we find her! That is the way she plans it, a good way to cover her operations, which is why we have not located her."

"She slipped up in leaving that list of names and addresses, and the book of matches behind," cut in Hilary.

"It is nothing on her though. That is probably what the girl came looking for, Peggy would have found it, knowing her. The girl was probably looking for either Peggy or the organization."

"We have it now," added Hilary with a smile. "We can use this list for indictments and subpoenas to the grand jury." Rex looks on with a smile shaking his head.

"What is wrong with that?" Hilary asked, a little confused, looking at Rex.

"Nothing, it's just that you want to get something on her so bad and catch her at it but she's too smart for that," Rex with a smile.

"And you don't want her caught; you would like for her to go free! Are you being honest in your statement, you do not know where she is?" retorted Hilary. "To me, she is just a material witness wanted for questioning, that is all for now, that I know of!"

"Captain, I would not make a false statement to the police and to be charged with making false statements, Peggy is not worth that! 'For now' you say until you can get something on her, which you have not been able. Yes, I am being honest about her; I do not know where she is and have told you that repeatedly! I am tired of this, when it is over, I am done with you, finished and tired of hearing this!"

"The FBI is not so sure; he wants to question you extensively about her and your relationship with her. I would advise you to get that cleared away, before you go on that trip to her parents or he might think you are involved, even hold you as a material witness! I am only trying to find answers to a whirl of confusion and mixed up investigation, I do not mean to harass you, believe me on that. "

"Are you serious?" Rex asked, surprised. "He thinks I am involved, how and why would he think that? Why would he think that?" Rex asked, suspicious of what Hilary might have said.

"He thinks you know more than you are telling to protect Peggy and that is why the organization is hell-bent on shutting you up. I have sort of wondered about that myself but you keep saying you are not involved," seeing Rex's suspicion and angry building.

"Well, I declare, I hardly know what to say, I open the door for you and the FBI, and now you think 1 am involved; you think I am withholding information? Why would I even bother to bring it up if I was stupid enough to withhold information! It does not make sense! I have not got to where to I am today by making dumb stupid mistakes like that, Borg might but I do not know if even he would not be that stupid! It would have to be for a darn lot greater reason than just a beautiful woman, for me to be that stupid! I thought you knew me better than that; I am not like that and that darn stupid. Bring on the darn FBI and let us get this darn thing cleared away; I will answer any darn question they want to ask me! However, no darn dragged out ordeal, I have to get back to my cases, and I am done and finished with you and the FBI! I thought you and I were friends but I see I was very badly mistaken! I will not forget this, and you can count on that! (Rex glaring at Hilary and Hilary seeing Rex is dead serious) Bring on them and let us get this over with for good, but no dragged ordeal! I will not forget this; you can count that, buster! You have nothing on your detectives far as smartness, you overlooked the burlap package as well, but I saw it!"

"I am sorry to have upset you so and get you so worked up but I am relaying my conversation with the FBI Director, John Cotter. He feels you possibly know more than you are telling or more than you realize you know. He feels that is why the Militia Organization wants you dead, he wonders about your relationship with Peggy also."

"You wander about me also, you just said so, is it possible he wants to question and grill me to see what 1 know for the organization? Have you even bothered to think about that? I think it is possible for that reason that he wants to grill me! Have you bothered to check him out, I can answer that, NO you have not!"

"Do you really think he could be for the Militia, you really think that? I guess it is possible, but I doubt it," Hilary said. Rex is still very angry and their friendship is in grave question, very possible shreds now by pressing him beyond limits.

"I told you everything I know and can think of, I have made that perfectly clear, at least I thought so; but that is not good enough for you! Did they find that truck that was used to ram me or have you bothered to look, too busy grilling me?"

"We have tried to find it but have not as of yet, but we will keep looking. The FBI located Max Guinean's apartment suite; nice and expensive too, not like his house. They went and searched the place but did not find anything. It was apparent that someone had got there first and cleaned house real good!" replied Hilary nervously.

"That figures, when did they go?" Rex asked, still tensed and very angry. "I thought he could not afford more than a house like he had, the way his house and he looked. They went together from appearance!"

"They went there when they found out who he really was," replied Hilary quietly. "The house was used as a cover for his apartment suite."

"Well, I am not withholding anything and far as possibly knowing something without realizing it. I do not know about that. I have told you everything I can remember and think off," Rex stated angrily, trying to think and remember of anything he might have discarded or overlooked. "I seriously wonder about John Cotter! I feel there is something; a mole is there somewhere if not him! If he is not the mole, then he needs to look under his own 'bed.'"

"Well, he wants to question you, he was firm about that."

"Bring him on and let us get it over with for good! I seriously feel he needs questioning too,   the way you just grilled me! What about going to check out the art gallery, get all of this over with so I can get back to my cases and a normal life if that is possible."

"Maybe tomorrow we could go there. But for the rest of today, you need to rest and calm down. (Rex smirks at that.) You really were angry there, which I did not intend to happen. I am so sorry to get you worked up and I will not press you again about Peggy. You could watch her house to see if anyone comes back. If you do see someone, call immediately and we will get a couple of detectives over there in a hurry," stated Hilary. "If nothing happens, watch TV, rest and relax for the rest of today."

"After the 'State Security' grilling I just went through today, I will try!" Rex replied without looking at Hilary, still tensed and very angry. "Forget about Peggy's house, I will be going to my backyard!"

"I am sorry about the grilling, really. I hope we can still be friends, but I am sorry." No reply from Rex. Hilary leaves, wondering how he is going to win Rex's friendship back; I really need his observation and knowledge. Nevertheless, Hilary feels he and Rex are through when this is over.

As the day wore on, it was just another day with nothing on TV except soap operas which Rex considered a total waste. He fixed a bunch of sandwiches and with a container of cold sweetened ice tea and a glass went to the backyard to 'rest and relax.' Finishing the sandwiches, he sat back in his lounge chair to relax with the ice tea when he heard the front door bell. "Who could that be, darn Hilary back already?

If it is. Immediately after seeing it was not, he called Hilary to say someone was at his front door, a man in a suit and a woman.

"Okay, wait three minutes before answering the door, that should give enough time to get somebody over there," replied Hilary, anxiously.

Rex slipped into his study and took a .375 magnum from the desk drawer, shoved inside his shirt and waited three minutes. Going to the door, they were gone. Looking up and down the street, there was no sign of them. Rex called Hilary back to say they had left and the cops had not arrived yet. Rex smirked.

"That figures. Did you see their faces?"

"Yes. I did, you think there might be a mug shot of them?" Rex asked doubtfully. "So much for the 'rest and the relaxation' that I was supposed to be getting, that the doctor ordered!" Rex scoffed.

"There might be a mug shot of them if we are lucky, if not, you could describe them to our artist. Sorry about your rest and relaxing."

"I figure I will be describing them to your artist, maybe I can rest and relax after the FBI and along with the grand jury and the federal trial! I will need it."

"You are probably right about the artist, but you never know. They will be back being that you didn't answer the door."

"To put a tap on my phone or rig something up in my house, as long it isn't a bomb, hopefully," added Rex nervously.

"We will keep your house under surveillance," said Hilary solemnly.

"But don't make it too noticeable or they won't come back, maybe that would be good? I guess they don't have anything to do but to check on me!" Rex smirked.

"I told you that they want you dead to shut you up about something and the FBI as well as I are convinced of it, but we wonder what?"

"Well, whatever it is, I wish it would come to light to get this over with and I can have a 'normal' life!"

"We would like that too: we're not enjoying this even though you think we are. I would enjoy going back to taking care of routine minor traffic and domestic offenses." Rex puts the ice tea in the refrigerator to keep fresh.

At the police precinct, Rex looking at mug shots for over an hour but failed to see anyone like the couple at his door or even a resemblance of them. He then describes them as the artist constructs their faces on paper. The FBI and Interpol had nothing.

"Tomorrow morning, I think we should go to the art gallery and have a look around," stated Rex. "We might as well, they have their goons out looking everywhere: the sooner this is over I will be able to get back to my cases and a normal life, hopefully."

"You're right, you might as well, whether you sit down and wait or actively pursue this, either way: they're after you for something you're not aware of. They want to get to you before you become aware of whatever it is and before you go before the grand jury."

The next morning. Rex calls Hilary to see if he is ready to go to the art gallery to look around or if he is too busy. Hilary had given Rex a separate number direct to his office, which went direct to his pager if he is out of office, bypassing the office switchboard and Sergeant Judy Sturgis' desk phone. Captain Hilary wanted to keep his secretary ignorant of Rex's physical, mental condition and as to where he was, just in case someone tried to get any information from her. If Rex called Hilary's office using this number, Sergeant Judy would not answer the phone. Captain Hilary's pager going off, he looked to see who is calling.

"What is new now?" Hilary asked weary of any more phone calls.

"What do you say we go to the art gallery and look around this morning instead of this afternoon? It is dull around here with no wheels to go anywhere; I am not used to this. I know how your detectives felt, just sitting around."

"You are supposed to be resting and relaxing for another month, remember?"

"Yeah, well, I am about to go nuts. I cannot take resting, and doing nothing for a whole month, I am not used to this. The stress I have been put through, I have not been able to rest!"

"Okay, I will be by shortly and we can go look," replied Hilary. Rex is not one for sitting around doing nothing; he likes to be busy doing something useful and being on the go! That is good, it shows ambition, not lazy, Hilary thought. "I can hear you smiling," Rex declared.

"You like me confined, I want to hurry up, get the 'SS' interrogation over with and convict these culprits of the militia so I can get my life back to normal," Rex stated on the way to the art gallery. "1 want to get back to my standing cases and do something useful."

"You being confined has been a change (Hilary smiling) but you feel you can just go back to the life you had, once they are convicted and in prison?" Hilary ignored the slur to "SS" interrogation. "Even if they are in prison, there will be a contract on you for sure then! You will probably have to move out of state and change your career as well your name and lifestyle," Hilary wondering if Rex could handle that.

"If that is the way it is to be, then bring it on, but me making a change to what? Being a private detective is all I have ever known, it is what I looked forward to, and I have trained for as my career. What else is there that I could do and do well? That will be a challenge!"

"I don't know what you could do, you may have to take training and learn a new career, you have been a big help in this investigation as well other cases; your knowledge and observation will be missed. You have enough funds to live on until you learn a new career?"

"Yes. I suppose so, my house is paid for, I could sell it and buy another somewhere, I have funds put away and investments," Rex said, thinking of moving.

"It might be better to live in an average priced apartment, condo, or townhouse or even a manufactured home in a park for a while, say for a year then move somewhere else," advised Hilary thinking of Rex, which would be a real change for him!

"That would be a real change alright (Rex wondered if he could do that), I am used to having a nice house and backyard to relax in and have a cookout," replied Rex.

"A contract hitman would be looking for something like that, a nice quiet plush neighborhood, more than likely, that is why a change would be good. I sure wish I could afford a nice house like yours."

"True, but starting a new career will be a real change and challenge! My present job paid for my house, which is why starting a new career will be a challenge."

"You have any idea what we are looking for at the art gallery?" Hilary asked as they came within sight of the art gallery. "I interrupted a judge's breakfast to get a search warrant."

"I suppose he was happy to see you?" Rex joked. "No, I figure it has been pretty well cleaned out with Peggy in charge. Even if she wasn't there to oversee it, but they might have overlooked something if we are lucky," admitted Rex.

They started looking room by room and finding nothing, the paintings, etchings, and prints all gone. Rex reaches the backroom, which is empty, the shipping crates gone leaving print marks. Peggy did a good job of cleaning the place out, no surprise to Rex. Hilary looks at Rex vexed and disappointed.

"Well, the only place left to look is the basement," Rex said, almost ready to give up. The basement was just as empty as the upstairs. Over on the wall next to a phone jack plug-in is a phone number almost rubbed out. Rex called Hilary over, to see if Hilary could trace what is left of the number.

Hilary runs over and Rex asked, "You think you could trace what is left?"

"We will work at it until we do," Hilary replied smiling and feeling relieved. "We will feed this partial of a number into the computer and see what it comes up with: maybe forensics can trace it? Any more good ideas you can think of?"

"Not at the moment, but I have to contact my insurance to find out when I can get a car."

"They know of the restrictions. So they are not going to cover you until these restrictions are lifted, you cannot even buy a car without insurance to cover it. Driving under those restrictions and not having insurance is a ticket violation offense, which would raise your insurance rates to 'high risk' even if you could get a car. You should know that!" Hilary lectured.

"I cannot sit around the house day after day doing nothing, I will go nuts. I understand how those detectives felt."

"So do I, but that is the price of a stakeout, get a hobby, besides I would enjoy having a house like yours. But I cannot afford a house that nice and not in that neighborhood!"

"Oh, I enjoy it and I am happy with my house and neighborhood. I enjoy the backyard and having a cookout, but sitting around the house all day long is not for me: there is nothing on TV but soap operas which I consider a total waste. Sitting around and not working is not making me any money," Rex replied. "I have to keep working to keep that house insured, taxes paid and afford my lifestyle. I need to keep moving! Far as a hobby, that would keep me occupied for a short while."

"Your house and lifestyle require money alright, but a short while is all that would be needed, until those restrictions are removed and I can understand you have to keep working. Having that house, I would too! For now, write a book about your experiences and cases, just change the names, times and places. That should prove interesting!"

"I could do that, I guess. But some cases would have to be classified and remain totally secret," Rex replied, thinking.

On arriving home, Rex had a feeling something was not right. He started looking around, starting to use the phone. He decided to check it first. Turning it over, it looked okay, unscrewing the base cover with a pock-etknife, inside was a button-size electronic bug. Rex replacing the base plate cover went to the neighbor, Ned Burley's house to use his phone.

"Hilary, arriving home, I had a feeling something wasn't right. Checking the phone, I discover a button-size electronic bug on my phone. I am wondering what other surprises are waiting me. You think you could send someone over to scan my house and see what else they planted on me?"

"Oh sure, where are you now? not at home I hope."

"No, I'm next door. The white house with green trim and shutters, small back porch."

"Stay there, we will be there shortly." Ten minutes later, the bomb squad and two detectives arrive in unmarked cars and street clothes, and take an electronic scanner into the house. Checking the phone, the electronic bug was a listening device, to send any conversation to a third party. Checking the rooms, there was an electronic bug under an end table in the living room, one under the bathroom sink, and one under the nightstand in the bedroom; all three to listen to any conversation in the house, all of the electronic bugs removed quietly. However, there was no bomb and no triggering device to cause a fire or gas leak.

"By removing these electronic bugs, they will know somebody is here," Lieutenant Ottoman stated.

"Yes. I know," replied Hilary worried, but where could Rex stay if not here? "They will be around. We could wait and arrest them after they get inside, hold them for breaking and entering, and electronic spying, while we interrogate them about their activities and who they work for."

"That is an idea, if they don't shoot up my house before entering," worried Rex.

"That would draw attention to them though, which I don't think they want: they will want to do their business and leave quietly," replied a bomb squad officer. "We better get rid of those cars though: I figure they will be around here shortly if they are going to come."

"Yeah. You are right, you guys go move those cars down the street, quick, and get back here," Captain Hilary turning to his officers and two detectives. One officer stayed with Hilary and Rex, the others got up and quickly moved the cars a block down the street. Running back, the detectives started griping about the special treatment given to Rex.

"You would think we're some sort of servant catering to royalty, the special treatment Hilary gives to Rex," gripped Larry Ottoman.

"Oh, you noticed that too, just because he stumbled onto that mysterious Peggy Lausanne and we didn't find that burlap package shoved under the bottom basement step and the book of matches under the snack bar. Too bad we couldn't find those instead of him," stated Nick Nelson.

"Some guys have all the lucky breaks, but I heard he found a number of other things as well, like the partial phone number in the basement of the art gallery and the bug on his phone. How did you people miss all of that? I heard he has gone to college majoring in a number of courses, as well service in the army, FBI, CIA and he attends seminars regularly for detectives," stated Ned Spooner, the bomb squad officer. "Well, the Militia organization is after him, and not us. And look at his neighborhood; I can't afford to live in here."

"Yeah, I know, he is well qualified, but do you think we will ever receive that kind of treatment he gets?"

"Not unless we stumble onto something big like Rex did, it's like he has a sixth sense or something for that kind of stuff! How did he know to check his phone?"

"Yeah, I heard he does real well as a private detective and he needs to be to afford a house in here. Well, he is a target and most likely go into protective custody and changing his name, address and kiss his career good bye," added Nick, smiling.

"If special treatment means that kind of life, living under fear of death, I think I can do without it; they almost got him in that accident, that was close"

"Yeah, it does have its drawbacks, doesn't it? an expensive price, giving up his lifestyle and this house. What a waste!"

Just a short while after the detectives and officers had gone back in the house, the door closed: a car came slowly down the street, with two men in the front and in the back, looking at Rex's house. Hilary, the detectives and two officers, and Rex stayed out of sight of the windows. The men went down the street, stopped for about five minutes.

"What are they doing?" asked Ottoman.

"Debating what to do I guess, maybe calling for instructions?"

"Now they're coming back."

"Take your places where they can't see you and get ready!" Captain Hilary ordered.

Turning around, they came back and pulled into Rex's driveway. Getting out, they started looking in the windows, then gathering at the front door. Staying out of sight, everybody stayed ready to pounce as soon as the men were inside. Picking the door lock, the men moved inside the living room, one going over to phone to check it while the others looked on. After he took off the base plate cover, Hilary, two detectives, two officers, and Rex leapt out with guns drawn.

"POLICE, YOU ARE UNDER ARREST, PUT YOUR HANDS UP, NOW!" Captain Hilary ordered.

Realizing the police had the drop on them and they were outnumbered, they angrily put their hands up while Ottoman frisked them for weapons and then handcuffed them.

"Yeah. We already removed all of the electronic bugs, including the one in the phone," stated Hilary, and then quoted their rights to them under the law while Nick called for a police van to come and take them to the precinct for questioning.

The officers took the suspects to the van, their guns tagged and left with Captain Hilary. Seeing a police van in Rex's driveway, the neighbors were out and watching. ABC and NBC News with their camera crews were there within a few minutes after the police van arrived, to get it all on film for the evening news.

"Where did you come from, who called you?" Hilary demanded, going over to Jan Roberts and the ABC camera crew. Rex stayed inside, in case somebody out there had a gun and waiting.

"Someone called and gave us a tip," replied Jan, smiling. "What's up with Rex Morgan's house, Captain?" "These men were caught 'breaking and entering' Rex's house!"

"A nice neighborhood like this, imagine that. How is the investigation coming along? Any information on 'Rex's condition' and where is he?" Jan inquired, looking at the house with a knowing smile. NBC News was right there, recording every word and catching Jan's smile, then turning toward Rex's house.

"He's recovering, that's all I'm willing to say!"

"He wouldn't happen to be inside, would he?" she asked with a knowing grin, then laughing. "Awhile back at the hospital he was pronounced dead from 'complications due to the concussion surgery.' Now, you say he's 'recovering.'"

"I'm not saying where he is and when he will be home, you babbling everything on the news isn't helping our investigation!"

"It's our job to report the news, freedom of the press, Captain! When will you say where he is?" asked NBC News reporter. Harold Jabots.

"Not today, that is for sure! I don't know when, maybe when you start helping our investigation instead of hindering it!"

"It's our job to report the news and your job to chase the suspects," replied Jan, laughing. Captain Hilary tells her he doesn't need her to tell him his job, he knows his job and then goes back inside Rex's house perplexed as what to do now.

"Captain Hilary knows where Rex Morgan is but he's not talking, I think I know too" (Jan and the camera crew looking at Rex's house). "Awhile back when Rex was injured in a 'hit and run' Captain Hilary and the hospital claimed he died due to complications in a concussion surgery on the brain, but now he says Rex is recovering but won't say where," Jan stated, smiling and looking at Rex's house suspiciously, the camera crews turned toward Rex's house as well.

"You're a target for sure now, Jan saw right through our secret of you being here. It would be too risky for you to stay here now, they know you are alive and here! They might spray your house, hoping you are inside or wait for you to come out. We've got to move you now," Hilary spelled out to Rex.

"Yeah. But where am I to move to?"

"We'll put you somewhere until we find a place. We have to! Both news reporters know you are in here from the way they looked at your house and the militia organization will too," replied Hilary.

"Sounds exciting. I like good food." Rex joked, nervously.

"No promises, I can't promise food like Samboa's but it will be decent, they're going to be watching and looking where we would move you to," Hilary cautioned. "They know you are here but they figure we will move you being it is out and we do not have a choice. They will be checking the places we would move you to and that you like. Nevertheless, they will keep checking here to make sure. We have to move you to somewhere they would never think of, wherever that is. We may have to put you someplace that isn't exactly your taste and style." Hilary grinning and wondering if Rex could cope with that.

"Oh, I realize that and I see your grin."

Rex replied, "I just hope it's only temporary, but where?"

"That, I don't know just yet but it will have to be some place other than here."

Back at the police precinct. Hilary getting tired of all this, started grilling the suspects to see who would break first and start talking, hopefully. The police had already taken the suspects' mug shots and fingerprints: compare them to those on file. There was nothing helpful, just minor offenses that probably would not even be concerned in a major court trial.

"Who are you working for, and who sent you? We can do this either the easy way or the hard way: which it will be rough; I grant you that!" Hilary declared. No reply but they were surprised to see Rex, no trace of his injury. "You will answer our questions, you are under arrest for 'Breaking and Entering, Electronic Spying' and you can be held for 'Withholding information to an on-going investigation' of Max Guinean, known as Luke Leprous, disappearance of Anne Towers, known as Peggy Lausanne: and her connection with the Militias Militia organization," stated Hilary angrily. "Also, add onto that the obstruction of an ongoing investigation!"

"We don't know what you're talking about," said the person who unscrewed Rex's phone.

"Who are you then and why did you 'break and enter' Rex's house?"

Hilary snared, looking hard at Karl Virgos. "Are you the leader or spokesman?"

No reply, the men just sat there occasionally looking at Rex surprised he survived the "hit and run," and showing up here.

"You recognizing Rex Morgan, you know something! There is the possibility you could be charged with 'withholding information vital of a hit and run' and accessory to attempted murder of a federal witness (pointing to Rex), if you do not talk. It is in your best interest to talk now and tell us what you know and whom you work for, it will go easier on you! If we turn you loose, the Militia will think you spilled your guts and talked. And we will let on as if you did to get off easy, if we turn you loose. On the other hand, we turn you over to the FBI, but they will not be so easy on you, I grant you that! They work different than we do," Hilary stated in a sinister voice. Nevertheless, there was no reply, no response. Their attorney, Amos W. Whittler walked in and said they were through until he had had a chance to talk with them.

With a smirk, Hilary said "go ahead and talk, but they're not going anywhere!" Maybe they will break easier if we question them separately, Hilary wondered if they would not talk, what would happen if we released just one of them: we would put the word out on the street that he spilled his guts talking. He would become a target but maybe the others would start talking. We would put an electronic bug in his shoe sole or the hem of his clothes to track them and see where he goes and to whom.

"When is the grand jury going to start their inquiry? I'd like to get going and get it over with and with the FBI too. If they think I am scared to face them and their grilling, they are crazy! Bring it on!" declared Rex.

"I don't know, the FBI has acquired all the names of board members, membership, employees, and sources of the organization and records," replied Hilary. "The FBI went back to that bank where Luke Leprous had a safety deposit box and opened it. He had a letter listing all of them, including the confidential backers, telling of their activities that he knew of, in case something happened to him. This is hard cold evidence that they can use in the grand jury; and to get their subpoenas. I don't know if they will use all of them to testify but this is enough for indictments for all of them! Anne Towers had good reason to flee, she was the bookkeeper and accountant, but it takes time for something this big."

"Anne embezzling the organization and being the head bookkeeper and accountant, she is definitely a target," stated Rex.

"She keeping the financial records for them, she could answer a lot of questions. She embezzling the organization as you said, that is why the militia wants her dead. I also checked out the FBI Director, John Cotter, to see if he is involved with the organization, he was surprised I would question his character and record and he was amused that you would suspect him but in a way, he understood. Far as I can tell, he is one of the good guys," replied Hilary.

"John Cotter could be one of the unlisted secret members, unlisted and confidential hacker, or sympathizer of the organization! Ah, you made a big break through, you have them on the 'hot seat' now with that list of names. I will be glad when it is finished! And I still suspect John Cotter!"

"Me too, I'll be glad when it's finished. It is rough trying to protect someone from hit men when you don't know who they are, it's nerve-wracking! I am putting my life on the line trying to shield you. You will always be a target though, even if they go to prison. Nevertheless, you have opened doors on a number of cases, but this is the biggest and most dangerous one yet I would say, but it will more than likely cost you your career as a private detective. You will have to change your career and most likely your lifestyle and name as well to stay alive," stated Hilary with a frown of acceptance. "Along with the bigger cases comes bigger risks."

"It's been an experience, sometimes interesting, sometimes dangerous and sometimes downright irritating," admitted Rex thoughtfully. "You could get Borg to take my place."

"Please, spare me the humor right now," replied Hilary.

"Well, I'm getting my fifteen minutes of fame."

"Oh, you're getting that alright," Hilary chuckled.

Checking around at the precinct, there was a detective in the Vice Squad who had a nice cottage upstate he had not used in over a year: he had been too busy remodeling his house and with his job as a detective, he had no time to go up there. Sitting back off the road a quarter of a mile, so quiet you could hear anything that moved. There was a creek close by that crossed the back part of his property: a very quiet, peaceful remote place to get away. I need a place like this, Hilary thought. It was a place where you could go to relax and rest your mind, and to take a break from life's stress, and unwind, let the world pass on by.

"I don't want it shot up in a gun battle," Jason Coatis declared.

"I can understand that alright, I wouldn't either, a nice place like that!" Hilary chuckled.

At the police precinct, Hilary calls the FBI Director, John Cotter and informs him that now the organization knows Rex is alive and even tried to contact him at his home. In addition, the ABC and NBC News were there to cover the arrest of the suspects and Jan Roberts practically spelled it out that Rex was there. The FBI Director said, "Yeah, I saw it on the news."

"Rex has to be moved immediately," Hilary said. "If you wish to question him, you have to do it before he moves or else you forget it!" Hilary declared.

"Wait just a minute here: you have to make available him for questioning whenever we need him! You are not dealing with some local police precinct; we are the FBI, and I don't think you want to challenge our authority to question him, I hope you understand that!"

"I'm not challenging your authority to question him, I am concerned about his safety, and I am putting a time on you to do it because of his safety! If I wait around for your convenience, he will be a sitting target! Rex staying here any longer puts his life in danger, understand that!" Hilary countered, angrily.

"It's your responsibility to protect him but we have to question him! Go ahead and move him, but make him available for questioning, either where you'll be hiding and feel safe or have him meet us somewhere," Cotter stated.

"When will that be? I feel it would be better to meet somewhere, someplace safe and of my choosing!"

"I'll have to schedule an appointment and get back to you."

"Make it quick, and don't ake all day!" snapped Hilary.

"I'll get back with you: we got a search warrant and stormed that organization's headquarters, seizing all of their documents and records. Maybe that will make you feel better: you're in an ugly mood!"

"I have reason to be, and it's about time you did something other than sit in your office, I'm down here in the 'trenches' while you're safe in your office! What 'reason' did you use to present to the judge, which judge did you get?" Hilary inquired.

"U.S. District Judge Joseph K. Hoffman, we stated that the organization had not registered with the federal government, nor had they declared their source of income or how much they were taking in," John Cotter replied.

"That's good, I'm glad to hear it, you're finally starting to move a little bit," breathed Hilary. "It took long enough!"

"Something this big takes time, you don't rush into an operation this big or you'll overlook something."

"Yeah, I know but we don't want to give them time to cover things up and create a new set of books and records either!"

After a few weeks from the first visit, the doctor examining Rex had declared him fully recovered far as he could tell. Rex packed two suitcases and an overnight bag; it was loaded into a plain unmarked car with dark-tinted windows, inside Rex's garage. Rex getting in the car, everything locked down tight: and the silent alarm turned on. Inside the house, motion video cameras were set up in most unsuspecting places.

It was a three hour ride upstate with the beautiful countryside, one stop to eat lunch and stretch, then on to the cottage. The cottage in the midst of woods with a running creek nearby was a nice and most relaxing setting, with the smell of outdoors and the soft breeze, three bedrooms, bath and half, nice kitchen and living room, a large deck off the back and a porch across the front. The woods around the cottage cleared twenty yards, both the front- and backyard, and ten yards on each side, except a couple trees in the front yard and one in the backyard.

"So the FBI managed to get the books before they were destroyed. Have they been 'doctored' or 'fixed?'" inquired Rex, suspicious.

"That will be studied and determined, do you think they have been or if there is another set of books and these were just there in case the Feds did raid the place? You feel these books and records have been messed with or they're not the real thing?" Hilary asked, uneasy with Rex's suspicions but felt he just might be right.

"Yes I do. I feel the organization figured the Feds might show up someday with a search warrant and take everything. I feel they figured it would happen eventually and were prepared. The Feds will need a real good bookkeeper/accountant to detect the 'fixes' and where things don't add up," added Rex.

"John Cotter will love hearing that," Hilary sighed sourly, despondent, realizing Rex might be right.

"Sorry, just have him prepared, check the accuracy of the books and records, compare one against the other over and over, looking for things that don't tally out, that don't agree with the other books and records. Do not leave any of them alone by themselves as a cautionary measure; it will take time. Don't take anything for granted."

"Borg brought in his Vista statement and the copy of the charge slip at the art gallery. We now have Peggy's signature, only her name is Anne Towers."

"She can change her name, her signature and writing like changing shoes and her face, if she hasn't already," Rex stated.

"True, but if she ever uses that signature or writes like that on a charge slip again, we'll be able to trace her," Hilary countered. "Stop trying to shoot down my positive spirit and hopes."

"Just facing the truth and facts as they are, I'd rather not get my hopes up than to have them shot down," Rex replied with a grin.

Hilary looks at Rex grinning and looks away. "If she uses that signature again, it will be for a purpose and reason."

"You're a real bundle of joy," Hilary said, sourly and Rex continues grinning.

"Sorry," replied Rex, laughing. Hilary says "ha-ha" and looks away at the woods, listening to the running creek.

"Enjoy this place, I wish I could, I'd love to have a place like this to get away." Hilary moaned looking around wishfully.

"Yeah, every working man needs a place to get away to, once in a while."

Back at the precinct, Hilary getting back to the FBI Director, John Cotter, relayed Rex's suspicions concerning the books and records, which the Director admitted with a groan, was possible.

"He really knows how to shoot down a guy's hopes, doesn't he? Tell him thanks a lot! Well, I wondered about that but I pushed that thought away, it is too depressing. Have him to be ready and meet me at 11:30 day after tomorrow to answer some questions about his relationship with the Miss Anne Towers, what he knows and saw at her art gallery, and about the organization. See how he feels about that!" Cotter shot back.

"Okay, but my officers will be with him at all times!" Hilary declared. "Where do we meet? Rex is ready: he says he only knows about her as Peggy Lausanne, nothing more. He wants to get this done and over with, no dragged out ordeals: that is his very words."

"Okay. I'll go along with the officers being with him but I don't know how long the questioning will take until I question him! We can meet at one of my offices or one of yours, unless you know someplace safer and better."

"Sounds good, one of your offices will do but don't tell anyone we're coming or which office it will be, Rex suspects a mole within the FBI," Hilary replied.

"Okay, but he is silly to think there might be a mole here," Cotter replied. "There better not be! Is there anything else he suspects?"

"It's better to be safe than sorry."

The next morning, Rex got up after a good night's sleep with the sounds of the outdoors and the creek running, had a good hardy breakfast, and with a mug of coffee, went out on the porch to relax and enjoy the scenery, listening to the birds singing. After sitting on the porch for a couple of hours or so, he explored the woods surrounding the cottage. The glory and beauty of nature in its all-natural beauty, I love it!

"Oh I had a nice dinner on the deck, a good night's sleep with the sounds of the outdoors, had a good hardy breakfast, took a mug of coffee out on the porch to enjoy and relax; then 1 went for a walk in the woods, exploring around the cottage," Rex teased.

"Don't rub it in," Hilary replied gruffly. "Tomorrow morning, you're to meet with the FBI Director, John Cotter for some serious questioning at one of his offices. So get up early and have your 'good hardy breakfast' and don't sleep in!" Hilary replied sourly.

"Are you jealous, Captain?" Rex asked, grinning. "You sound like it."

"Yes, I am jealous and I can hear you grinning!"

The next morning Rex got up early, had another hardy breakfast, washed the dishes, and got ready to go for the interrogation at the FBI Building. Hilary arrived at the cottage with four plain-clothes officers, asked Rex if he had his "hardy breakfast."

"Yes I did, I have enjoyed this place. What is the vest for, playing safe in case there is a sniper?" Rex asked jokingly already knowing the answer. Hilary and the officers already had theirs on. "A smart sniper will figure that and go for the head instead."

"It's for you in case there is one, at least your body will be safe, hopefully a sniper won't figure that; we'll have to be extra watchful." Rex agreed with that.

The drive hack to Berkeley was smooth and the countryside nice until you got within sight of town. Then it was roadside signs and billboards, and houses! Pulling up in front of the FBI Building, just as Rex was getting out, a man with a cap pulled low across the street, started firing at Rex and the officers. Rex dropped down quickly but the officers didn't move fast enough, one catching a bullet in the back of his neck, almost at the base of his skull, hitting the spinal artery and the other officer catching a bullet behind his head. The shooter took off running, realizing he had failed his mission, with the other two officers in hot pursuit. Catching him eventually and slamming him against the wall of a store, frisked and cuffed, and brought back in total disgust, his rights were being quoted to him. The officers found his pistol, a .9 mm Lugar, tossed between two store buildings.

The Medical Examiner and Crime Scene Specialist arrived within a few short minutes, the crime scene closed off. The Medical Examiner examined the slain officers, made his report, and said he would go into more details in his lab. The Crime Scene Specialist surveyed and recorded the crime scene. Then ABC and NEC News arrived to cover the scene and get the lowdown of why the questioning of Rex and just missing the shooting, asked a bystander what happened. He told the reporters that two officers had been shot, the sniper caught and taken inside the FBI Building.

"Anything you want to say on the capture of the sniper or are you still not talking, again?" Jan Roberts asked.

"I have told you before I can't disclose that, that is confidential and they just call! They do not give their name. You have nothing to say. Huh, still not talking!"

"You tell me who is calling you and be a little more cooperative, then I might consider being more cooperative, but not until then!"

Inside the FBI Building, "Who tipped you off we were coming?" Hilary demanded of the suspect, there was no reply. "You will talk; you killed two police officers and attempted to kill a federal witness! You won't walk from this!" Captain Hilary stormed. The suspect is in FBI lock-up but with the police officers keeping a tight grip and in police custody. Captain Hilary wanted John Cater to see this, a sniper waiting for them! Let him explain that!

ABC and NBC News seeing they weren't going to get anything from Captain Hilary, much less the suspect. The Medical Examiner and Crime Scene Specialist both said talk to Captain Hilary. The reporters gave a report of the shooting, killing two officers and an arrest of the suspect sniper, waited to see if there would be anything else. Now, it is on the news, Captain Hilary thought, the Militia will know the sniper failed. However, the sniper knows that the Militia will know he failed as well, maybe that can work in the police's favor as an advantage.

"So you don't have a mole, okay, explain how he knew we were coming, he shot two of my officers, killing them! The sniper stays with us, we do not know who your mole is yet, but he will tell us! Are you the mole, how did he know about us coming otherwise? Did you write it down or tell anyone? We have his pistol, a .9 mm Lugar! Explain that, if you can!" Captain Hilary yelled.

Cotter bewildered at the realization that there is a mole within the FBI and he is under suspicion possibly of being the mole until he can clear himself, he did not have any answers: just stood there mum, shaking his head in disbelief. "I don't know what to say, I didn't tell anybody, I didn't even write it down on my schedule! I just can't believe this!"

"Believe it, it happened! Excuse me. I need to make a phone call," Hilary said, getting his cell phone to call the Police Commissioner, Wayne Melton.

"You can use my phone in my office, it's a private line," Cotter said brokenly, sick of what has happened and maybe his career at stake.

"No thank you!" Hilary snapped and walked a few feet away, talking in almost a whisper.

"When you were talking to Hilary on the phone, were you using the phone in your office?" Rex asked, still a bit shaken up from the second attempt on his life. John Cotter just looked at Rex perplexed: he is questioning me instead of me questioning him! I cannot believe this! This is a hellish nightmare, John Cotter thought nervously.

"Well, yes but..."

"Then let's go check your phone; lead the way," Rex replied, looking at the director suspiciously. Hilary stood there glaring at John Cotter as if he was the guilty mole, making him nervous and weak at the thought of himself being a suspect. He knew how suspects feel now.

"You two officers keep him under constant guard and if he even tries to escape, brain him, anything more than breath, brain him!" Hilary ordered his officers, pointing to the sniper. "You made a bad mistake killing my officers, a very bad mistake! You will regret this!" Hilary stormed.

"You can count on us controlling him. Sir," the one officer said, both of them laughing, the sniper in a sweat and scared.

"Wait until I get through with this call," Hilary ordered, glaring at the director, this being on the news was really making him nervous and edgy.

Cotter feeling embarrassed and humiliated, realizing he is under suspicion and Hilary giving orders now until this cleared up, but Cotter knows he is innocent but not knowing what to do or say. Cotter led the way to his office, beginning to sweat which Rex and Hilary noticed. This may be the end of my career if it stops here, and this shooting is on the news now, Cotter realized. Internal Affairs will be putting all of us under a microscope to find the mole! I may end up on trial or under investigation unless this mess can be resolved soon.

Rex took Cotter's desk phone and unscrewed the mouthpiece and then the earpiece. There was nothing there that should not be there. "This is the phone you used?" Hilary asked, still angry and suspecting John Cotter of being the mole.

"Yes, but I don't understand."

"Could someone have been listening in on your line?" Rex asked looking outside Cotter's office door, a secretary nearby at her desk working.

"They could have but I was on a private line." That said, Rex had an idea, following the cord to a small hole in the floor.

"Where does this cord go?" Rex asked checking out his hunches, wondering if John Cotter was the mole or if his phone has been wiretapped. Internal Affairs could get right down mean and nasty when they want answers, and they will want answers in a case like this! This is an embarrassment and a black eye for the FBI!

"To the basement to a terminal," Cotter replied, worried that his career may be in ruins, feeling drained and stressed out but now wondering if Rex is onto something like his phone being wiretapped. "Repairs have been made before and an update of some new technical wiring down there but no problems since then."

"Yeah, someone may have created a problem outside and then pretending to be a repairman, put an electronic device on your line, so your calls could be picked up and listened to or intercepted by remote control from somewhere else," stated Rex.

"You say you've had repairs and a technical update lately?" Hilary asked, picking up at what Rex is getting at now.

"Yeah, the computer circuitry went down, repairs had to be made in the basement about three weeks ago. They made some adjustments on the phone line as well," Cotter replied.

"Very possible this time it was to wiretap your phone," stated Rex. "Who did you call?"

"The ATPT, same as always. The technicians on arriving were from ATOT Phone Company, which has always given most excellent service: they were the same guys as before, they acted a little nervous though, now that I think of it. They flashed their badges, no reason to suspect anything."

"Did you actually look at their badges, and then look at them; did the pictures match their faces, no alterations?" Rex asked.

"Yes the pictures matched their faces, a glance, we're really busy with calls, the switchboard was over-swamped with calls that day, and we were all very busy that day. I didn't have time to watch them: they didn't stay but just a few minutes anyway."

"Just as I thought, they meant for you to be busy, they probably arranged the phone calls so you couldn't keep a watch on them. It only takes a minute or so to place a wiretap on a line if they know their job. Where was your security during all of this?"

"There was a ruckus going on outside and the security had to make sure they didn't come onto our property and do something, it was over in a few minutes."

"They made your computers go down, or someone inside caused it and they arranged a disturbance outside to draw the security out there, all over in a few minutes. That is all they needed, a few minutes. Do you have a switchboard operator, how well do you know her?"

"Yes, we have one, but it couldn't be her, she has been with us for over twenty years now and as loyal they come. Janie Evers. She just makes sure everything runs smoothly," replied John Cotter.

"Let's look at the computer circuitry and check it out," said Rex, suspecting the Militia sent a couple of people to wiretap John Cotter's phone, and Captain Hilary wondering who did what. Going to the basement. Cotter pointed to the computer circuitry, Rex spotted the electronic device, he had learned about in the seminar. Rex removed it and checked the circuit, then reconnected the phone line. Cotter was embarrassed that he had been conned and duped so easily.

"Well, we have a shooter that we can get some answers out of as to who sent him," Hilary said in a determined mean-spirited voice, looking at the shooter in handcuffs, upon returning upstairs. "It's either the needle for him, or he gives us the answers we want if he wants off Death Row! The choice is up to him!"

"Providing you get your answers before he gets hit, look how close they came to getting me!" Rex added in.

"Thanks for the comforting thought, you're a 'Job's comfort,'" Hilary replied sourly realizing Rex was right.

"Just being realistic," Rex replied. "I'm sure there's another one around somewhere, I'm sure of it!"

"You're a real comfort and joy to be around, dangerous to be around too, I can see that. Are you ready to be questioned?" Cotter asked, hoping this is finished being that Rex found the wiretap.

"Before he says anything or answers any questions, I want to know the source of how this guy found out about us coming, traced and eliminated! That is a must, besides I think Rex has just proved himself!" Hilary angrily declared.

Stunned, John Cotter looked at Captain Hilary, "Oh, this place is still under suspicion and me too?"

"Until the source is traced and eliminated, yes, someone told the shooter we were coming and like Rex said there has got to be some mole here and I want to know who! Two good officers have been killed, this guy and whoever told him is facing the death penalty!" The shooter looks panicky, knowing his life span is very short right now. "Someone here is a mole and I want to know who!"

"The shooter and whoever did get the word to him will be charged with a federal offense! I think Rex is right, someone wiretapped my phone by an electronic remote control device at the terminal, to a third party, it had to be!" Cotter stated. "I also want to know who the mole is!"

"That is true, your phone was wiretapped but there still might be a mole here and he might have caused the shutdown, until that is traced and eliminated (Hilary looking at John Cotter), Rex doesn't answer any questions!" Hilary snarled. Turning and staring at the shooter and then Rex, said, "Let's go!"

"The mole couldn't have been from your police precinct, could it?" Cotter challenged.

"No, I have thought about that and taken another thorough look, checked, double-checked and crosschecked as well a profile review at my staff's background and records, and checking them out. Besides, they would not want to have to face me! I'm ready to go, I'm done here!"

ABC and NBC News crews gone and the shooter under tight security so he doesn't get shot on the way back to the precinct, Rex asked Hilary if he minded him observing the shooter during interrogation, I've had experience in that area and might be able to pick up something if he says anything or talks, expressions sometimes tell a lot."

"Oh yeah, that's right, you have had experience in observation and interrogation, you might pick or detect something. If he doesn't talk, he's facing the death penalty for sure and he knows that, killing two police officers and attempting to kill a federal witness," Hilary said. "You can observe but we'll have to do the questioning. I could definitely use your input and observation though."

"You put the scare into him back there at the FBI Building, he was panicky. I think he will talk if you take the death penalty off the table. Otherwise, he has nothing to lose by keeping quiet." Hilary just smiled.

"Even if he talks, tells everything he knows, it will be 'life without parole' under protection for sure. I feel that is as far as the District Attorney will go, killing two officers and attempting to kill a federal witness is a federal offense. I think if he talks or not he is a marked man, a target, especially now that it's on the news," Hilary stated.

"I agree and I understand that, the news babbles everything, hindering and obstructing the investigation, this time, let it work for you getting him to talk," Rex replied.

"Yeah, I like that."

At the police precinct, the shooter was processed, booked and his mug shot taken, and put in a holding cell for a while to think over his predicament. Taken into an interrogation room, he wearily sat down, depressed now arrested; and now facing the death penalty or life in prison if he talks, his life is over. He realized he would become a target if he talks or not and he was told ABC and NBC News had been there to report the arrest even though they did not get to see him. That would seal his doom, the Militia knowing he failed. Rex watched through a one-way observation window, looking at a very depressed and weary sniper. In a way, Rex rather felt sorry for him. Hilary walked in, sat a tape recorder on the table, to record the interrogation. At first, the sniper would not talk but finally gave his name, Barry Williamson, but that was all.

"Fine, don't talk, they will strap you down and put a needle in your arm, and that will be the end of you! We have your pistol, a .9 mm Lugar and they will compare the bullets taken from the slain officers to one from your pistol! I heard that ABC and NBC News have reported the shooting at FBI Building, they were there to report it! How long do you think it will take for the Militia to realize you failed?"

"If I talk, I'm dead!"

"Oh, you think if you don't talk they'll let you live?" Hilary asked with a smirking mocking grin. "You think we're going to say you didn't talk after killing two officers? No way, we will let on as if you did talk!

If we were to let you out of here, how long do you think you would live? They would think you talked and we cut a deal! They would shoot you anyway to keep you quiet!"

"You think you can protect me if I do talk when I almost got Rex Morgan?" Barry asked with a smirking grin. "I knew what he looked like before I even saw him! They can get to anybody if they want to!"

"They would find a way to get to me like I found a way to get to Rex: they would make it their business to find a way! A man gave me a picture of Rex."

"But Rex is still alive and unharmed from the shooting, even though it did cost a couple of officers' lives." Hilary replied. "Not even scratched, tell me who gave you the picture?"

"He is one lucky devil, no one seems to be able to get him, but I came close; however, he came even closer in that 'hit and run' and there was nobody to stop it!" Barry replied, ignoring the question.

"Yes, you came close and Rex did get hit in the 'hit and run' but he survived, and the person responsible is dead! Now, we have you, so what's it going to be, you talk or you take the needle?"

Another three hours, he broke down, he was paid $10,000 cash by a man he had seen two or three times, to kill Rex and he would get another $40,000 wired to his account if Rex was pronounced dead and confirmed; and he got away with it. He had met the man at an outside cafe off the college campus, where the picture of Rex was given to him, taken whenever, with the money.

"Where is the money now?" Hilary continued grilling.

"Tucked away somewhere safe, why? Are you going to take that away too?" Barry asked with a smile.

"You don't profit by crime, what good does it do you, going to prison for life? You can't spend it there, it could go for your upkeep in there," answered Hilary. "We have to pick out the man who gave you the picture and money, do you know his name? Was it John Cotter, the FBI Director at the FBI Building?"

"No, it wasn't Cotter, but I've seen him once or twice in passing at a short distance away. He was a little bit older than Cotter, with a touch of grey on the sides, around his ears, same build as Cotter. You will put me under protective custody?"

"Yes, you will be under protective custody. Where did you see him? Where did you see him?" Hilary asked, anxiously and wary of the answer.

"I saw him around the FBI Building, going in and coming out." That was like a bombshell, but expected.

"You saw him going in and coming out of the FBI Building?" Hilary asked, alarmed. Rex and his suspicions confirmed. This would most definitely bring in the Internal Affairs of the FBI to check everybody! Barry said the man was not Cotter. So who was it?

"That's right, surprising isn't it?" Barry smiled, seeing the look of alarm on Captain Hilary's face. "They find a way to get to you either by money in hard times or your family's safety or by blackmail. If they can't get you to cross over, they will remove you to keep you quiet!"

Rex listening was not surprised at someone being in the FBI, but having it confirmed was a real big surprise! Information about him coming had got out, but being that Barry said it was not Cotter, who was it? After that electronic device, he found it hard to suspect Cotter and now we know: it was not Cotter. From Barry's description, it should be easy to pick out the 'mole.'

"Are you sure about this, you're not putting me on, messing with me? In your predicament, you do not mess with me!" Hilary warned.

"Oh, I'm net messing with you: I was standing twenty feet away when I saw him! I having nothing to lose now, I am dead anyway now with the Militia knowing I failed! Surprising, you think you're safe with the FBI and then find out there's a mole among them!" Barry stated, grinning. "The FBI is supposed to be working with you but one of them is a 'turncoat' working with the other side!"

"You are being straight with me?" Hilary asked, uneasy and angry.

"Yes, I am being straight with you." Barry replied. "I have no reason to lie now, but not anymore."

"Excuse me, I will be back, this I have to report this to the Commissioner," Hilary stated, visibly shaken, walked out with the tape recorder. The mole is not John Cotter he said and he saw him; so who is he? "Rex, did you hear that? What do we do now, except take this to the Commissioner, Wayne Melton, and let him decide. He will undoubtedly call the Internal Affairs and let them take it from here, we cannot call the FBI just yet, and we do not know who the mole is. I had better take this to the Commissioner and let him listen to the tape; then decide what to do."

"That is all you can do, let him call the Internal Affairs, let them handle the FBI mole. You had better put him under real tight protective custody like me, just do not put us together, I still do not trust him entirely, check out his story before you embrace him, and let him point out the mole. With the word out of an arrest made, they will be after him and the mole might be on the run to avoid arrest. You certainly can't let anything else go to the FBI now!"

"Oh, I still regard him with suspicion too, but I feel he is telling the truth now," Hillary stated, taking the recorded tape of Barry Williamson's confession and statements to the Police Commissioner, Melton and let him listen. The Commissioner was stunned and alarmed hearing this, hardly knowing what to say. He said he would present this to the Internal Affairs; he made a copy just in case there was another mole in Internal Affairs. "Have him finger the FBI mole!" he ordered.

That evening, a report came in to Captain Hilary that John Cotter's wife came home from her job to find him in his study, at his desk, a hole on the left side of his head in the temple. The shot from a .44 Magnum Smith & Wesson. Perhaps the same bullet that killed Max Guinean fired by the same person? The lab was checking and comparing the bullets. Suicide ruled out, the angle was wrong; his height and sitting down, he was right-handed but the shot came from the left side, after being shot, the blood begin to settle in the position he was in. The shot at a downward angle of 2 feet went through the "dura mater" of the outer "membrane" and splintered the "pia mater" to the brain and spinal cord, blood splattered on his shirt and a bloody hole in the temple. Cotter must have known who his attacker was; he looked tensed and startled. Captain Hilary reading the report just shook his head in disbelief but was not surprised. It must be someone within the FBI aware of the meeting, decided to shut John Cotter up after he found out who the mole was.

Was he involved and knew too much or just found out who the mole was? John Cotter was not the one Barry saw going and coming out of the FBI Building. Barry said the man he saw and gave him the money and picture was a little older than Cotter. Apparently, Cotter found out who the mole was, but too late. Bewildered and shaken, Hilary wandered what is next. Who are the good guys and where are they? It is like the spy with no name and no face.

Internal Affairs called in to look at the entire FBI staff and personnel, checking and rechecking everyone's identity, and crosschecking files and background, no exceptions or favorites, everyone is to go under the FBI's microscope. Hilary and Rex felt they might even look at them and the police staff, until the mole is exposed and they know there are no more moles. Let them come on and check out the police force; if there is any, go ahead and weed them out! We will go after them! Larry Flippant, Director of Internal Affairs, known as one that lived and breathed by the law, the rules, with no exceptions! He carried the nickname, "The Head Hunter and he lived up to the name too!

The FBI Forensic Lab checking the bullets taken from the slain officers and compared to the bullet from the Lugar was a match. The FBI Lab under the watchful eye of Internal Affairs compared the bullet from John Cotter to the one from Max Guinean—was a match as well. The gunman who shot Max Guinean also shot John Cotter: he must be within the FBI Building here in Berkeley!

Mitch Miller, the Director of Operations under John Cotter and divorced with no children, apparently felt it was time to take a very long vacation, except Internal Affairs had figured on someone might want to skip the country. All of the airports, harbors, and bays around the country were under tight security; but Mitch figured they would be. They will be patrolling the highways and expressways as well. He packed three suitcases and his briefcase into the trunk of his car, and then started for the bank. From there, he would be on his way. He withdrew $80,000 claiming that he was "buying a yacht and the private owner prefers cash being he was going on a long cruise and stay in Europe," Mitch claimed.

Word of the large withdrawal transaction relayed to the bank manager and then to Internal Affairs, an agent of the bank and two FBI agents drove to his house to question him but he was already gone, as Mitch had planned. An APB posted on him to bring him back to Berkeley, California for questioning.

Checking Mitch's files, everything seemed in order, a search warrant was issued for his house. Copies of sensitive, secret "Office Use only" files of the ongoing investigation of the Militias Militia organization and Anne Towers, known as Peggy Lausanne were found in partial burnt ashes in the fire place but forensic could savage it through "refinery." Rex's address, phone number, and picture shoved under a desk drawer, almost hidden, a surprise he left all of this. The .44 Magnum Smith B. Wesson was not in the house. Realizing the warrant did not cover the garage or shed, a search warrant was obtained for those, the gun found wrapped in a burlap wrapper like the one found in Peggy's basement, on an upper support beam of the shed. He was in such a hurry to get away before getting arrested that he apparently forgot about the gun and taking time to finish burning the documents. The FBI Forensic Lab would raise it up enough to use as evidence.

Mitch Miller would be facing the death penalty, killing a federal FBI Director and a federal witness wanted for questioning and now fleeing as well. The dominoes at last were not beginning to tumble now, just a matter of time. Would we find Anne Towers alive? That also was a matter of time, alive and well, Rex hoped.

Mitch Miller arrested in the Pueblo Mountain of Oregon, brought back to Berkeley for questioning in the two murders he had committed. He had been hiding out under a cliff. Back in Berkeley, after being processed, fingerprinted and a mug shot taken, and then they presented the evidence against him. His attorney, Peter Tobeman, asked what was on the table as a plea bargain.

"What could you possibly have to interest us to offset the death penalty?" Assistant District Attorney Cheryl Nickles asked with a smirk. "You killed two people, the FBI Director and a federal witness fugitive wanted for questioning! Then you fled to avoid prosecution!"

"My client could tell you a lot about the Militias Militia organization and their activities."

"Oh can he really? What about their sources of income and associates, can he tell me anything about that as well?"

"I had no way of knowing that, I wasn't privileged to that information, you have to be a board member or maybe a financial sponsor to know that," Mitch replied.

"I don't know that this little bit of information would be enough to avoid the death penalty. Killing John Cotter, the FBI Director is a very serious offense and a federal fugitive wanted for questioning is a serious federal offense! You might be joining your friend, Barry Williamson, on Death Row!"

Mitch saying he had heard of Barry Williamson but never actually met or talked to him, Cheryl said she'd introduce him, she was sure they would have a lot talk about while there. Mitch said he could offer evidence in Max Guinean's murder of the U.S. Attorney General, Anthony Gilmore. It was a very big case back then.

"It was, back then but that is history now, unless you have something new and big to go with it, what else?" Cheryl insisted. "You give me what I want or you take the needle, it's up to you, either way won't bother me! What about the organization's procedures of illegal shipping and the smuggling, how do they smuggle people in and out of the country plus all the other stuff in and out of the country? Give up the names and routine procedures and those that are not routine as well! How do they work it? Write it all down, everything, leaving nothing out!" Cheryl shoved a legal pad and pen across the table to him. "What is it going to be, Mitch Miller?"

Mitch and his attorney looked at each other, the attorney leans over to consult with him silently. Turning to Cheryl Nickles he says. "In exchange for 10 to 15 years and a lifetime of secured protection?" This went on for another five minutes, Cheryl saying no, it is "life without parole" in exchange for the information or else the needle: she decides to break for lunch and unwind while Mitch and his attorney talk. Cheryl already had been told "life with no parole," if and only if he talks. Meanwhile, Mitch Miller's activities are further looked into and thoroughly investigated. After lunch, Cheryl Nickles returns and is ready to wind this up.

"Anthony Gilmore's murder. Max Guinean is dead and now we have Max Guinean's murder, your client (pointing to Mitch)! No, he gives me the information I want, in exchange for 'life in a secured prison with no chance of possible parole' for life!" Cheryl retorted. "That is it, nothing else is on the table, that is it and that is the way it is going to be!'

"That is no life, always the fear of being killed, afraid to eat because it might be laced, afraid to sleep, afraid to go out in the prison yard," Mitch stammered.

"You killed two people, a federal official, FBI Director, John Cotter and a federal witness fugitive, Max Guinean, am I supposed to feel sorry for you? Where is Peggy Lausanne or is it Anne Towers?" Cheryl smirks getting up from her chair.

"Okay, okay, but you've got the sweet job of protecting me and that won't be easy! She is Anne Towers far as I know and I don't know where she and her staff are, she is good at hiding! We haven't been able to find her yet."

"You're not lying: you don't know where she is? Don't lie to me if you're smart and you wish to live!" Cheryl persisted. "Tell the truth, you're not lying, you don't know where she is? I'm ready to walk out of here and leave you be, it won't bother me either way!"

"No, I am not lying," replied Mitch, growing weary and tired, seeing Cheryl not caring whether he lives or dies.

"You think real hard and give me this information I asked for plus a lot more or prepare to take the needle," Cheryl replied, getting up to leave the room.

"I don't know where Anne Towers and her staff are."

"Tell me what you do know and do not hold anything back!" Cheryl snapped, leaving the room.

"Boy, she is a hard one, a real witch, she said it wouldn't bother her whether I take the needle or not!"

"Yeah, she's a mean one alright, the trouble is she has you 'dead-to-right' and she knows it," the attorney replied. "She left no chance to negotiate; she's demanding the whole entire layout of the organization, names, places, everything. She wants it all. She is cold."

"I'm a dead man, just a matter of time. I know it. Even if I don't talk, the Militia will get me first and if they don't, I get the needle," Mitch stated, despondent.

"They're supposed to protect you, some way or another, it's their job to protect you."

"How do you stop an assassin's bullet from a rooftop of some tall building or a van from somewhere speeding by or some crazed sinister killer on the inside, waiting? Barry almost got Rex and he would have if those two police officers hadn't got in the way. They may not miss with me. They may hire someone outside the organization, someone unknown and with no record."

"Demand the best protection, put the burden of protecting you on them before opening up and talking."

"Sometime, that isn't enough, not with an unknown sleeper assassin in the wings, waiting," replied Mitch. "I don't know the assassins, their identities are kept top secret, they don't even know each other and there is no telling where they'll show up or when. Sometimes, they do their own planning when given an assignment and carrying it out. How do you guard against someone like that?"

"Put that burden on them, let them sweat it out," replied Peter Toberman, the attorney.

"They did with Rex Morgan but Barry still almost got him, I'm sure he gave them a scare and Rex too. They have arrested the assassin; but 1 don't know all the assassins the organization has. They're around somewhere, you can count on that!"

Outside the observation window, Cheryl Nickles was watching and listening along with the District Attorney, Harold Spellers, pondering the next move; Mitch and his attorney's comments weighing heavily on their minds. He had a darn good point, his safety rested with the FBI and the District Attorney's Office. How do you guard against something you cannot foresee, you know nothing about, and you do not even know who they are, where they are at or when they plan to strike until it happens? Arranging for Mitch to see Barry Williamson through the observation window, to make sure he knew Barry Williamson. Mitch seeing Barry was very surprised.

"Ah, you do know Barry Williamson, who is he in the Militia organization and what position does he hold?" Cheryl asked.

"He is a standing party member, and one of the most elite party enforcers, I'm surprised you caught him!" Mitch exclaimed.

"We caught him trying to kill Rex Morgan, a federal witness, but we have him now in our custody!"

"It's doubtful you'd have caught him if he had got away or disappeared! He has helped a whole lot of people disappear. He is a master of disguises and alias names. The way he works it, he lets them decide where they want to go but he does not ask, and they do not tell. That way, if he is caught, he doesn't know where they went or where they are."

"Well, we have him now, and thanks for letting us know about him." Cheryl said. "If you can hang onto him, he is a slippery one!" Mitch replied, smiling.

"Thanks for the warning!" Barry Williamson taken to a maximum-security cell, with his hands cuffed to a chain around his waist and to legs irons, was under constant watch day and night to wait for trial.

They strike your front door to draw your attention to the front while they come in the backdoor, or the backdoor plus the windows: or they line you up in the crosshairs of a sniper rifle with a scope. Where can we hide and hope to protect him until the grand jury and federal trial, then what? Which prison would feel and be safe enough? Not a populated prison, you would not know who is bad and who isn't. Inspecting at each meal would be for as long he lived. You can only do so much, but to protect this man, we must go beyond that! Some would say after he has told everything he knows at the grand jury and federal trial, and he is murdered then he deserved the death penalty anyway. Just keep in mind the next "Mitch" that has valuable information might not talk because as soon as he does talk and testify, he would end up like Mitch, no longer needed.

Later on, Mitch addressed that very issue, "What about after the grand jury and federal trial I have told everything, am I going to be protected or become a morgue stiff? How are you going to guard against an unknown assassin, someone you can't foresee?"

"We can't say how or what we'll do until we come to that situation, I realize we won't know who they are or will be, you have to help us there to survive. We'll have to play it by ear and be on the lookout for them," Cheryl stated.

"I don't know who the assassins are and if you wait for them to approach or attack, it will be too late, they are not going to announce or warn you! They will wait until you are least expecting them: your guard is down, no matter what it takes or whom it takes! They may use someone not associated with the Militia. It may be five or ten years or it may be two or three months, or next week. I feel they are busy right now planning something and waiting for an opening. There is no way that I know of who they will use or when; they may use a dozen, figuring one or two will get through to do the job; they would take down a hotel to get their prey! Someone may strike because of blackmail, a family member kidnapped and held as a life and death hostage," Mitch stated. "How are you going to handle or get around that?"

"You have some strong questions which I'm not prepared to answer right now, but I can say we will do whatever it takes, whatever we can. I don't have any answers right now..., but I will have as soon as possible."

"And yet, you want me to tell everything I know when you can't guarantee my safety? What do you take me for, a fool? You guarantee my safety and then I'll talk and only then!"

"No, we do not take you for a fool, but like the policemen who gave their lives to protect Rex Morgan our people put their lives on the line to protect you as well. You telling us about the Militia may help locate and arrest them."

"Yeah, the next assassin may be using a high-powered scope on a sniper rifle from a high building or a speeding van," Mitch countered. "You can part the hairs on a man's head with that!"

"We realize the effect of all of that, we'll be on the outlook for that, and our people will encircle you. We always do. Rex had four policemen with him."

Barry Williamson being handcuffed to a chain around his waist and then to leg irons, was put in an unmarked car, and taken to an undisclosed location under tight security. After four grueling hours of questioning and the same old old story all the way through, he pretended he didn't know anything more than who hired him. He just saw it as an easy way to more money than he had ever seen at one time; he hadn't counted on getting caught. It was doubtful that he would ever stay wherever they took him, always moving suspects as a cautionary measure while watching to see if anyone is following.

Cheryl informed him that Mitch Miller had recognized him as a long-standing party member of the Militia, one who helped others to flee custody of the law by disguise and alias names. Barry immediately denied knowing Mitch and the things he said, but soon on meeting him, his pretense fell apart in his facial expression. He knew it was over as well as Cheryl Nickles, looking at him smiling.

Rex Morgan back in the safety of the cottage where he was hiding out until the grand jury and federal trial, discusses with Hilary about going to see Anne's parents and sister, to see if they know anything of Anne's whereabouts or if she has even contacted them.

Captain Hilary feeling Rex really wants to find Anne, thought it best to let him go, he just might find her. However, unknown to Rex, two detectives would follow him not only for his own safety, but also to see if Rex really would actually fine her and hide her. So Rex wouldn't know he was being shadowed. Hilary had two detectives from his old precinct to tail Rex wherever he goes. Knowing where Rex is going, the two detectives are already at the airport and checked in when Rex gets there.

Flying to the state capital, Charleston, Rex goes to the Bureau of Births and Deaths, and identifies himself and requests the name of Anne's parents and sister. Rex stated that he needed to contact them regarding Anne. They live in Corinne; he was given their address; Anne's sister, Roxann, lives at home. Arriving at the address, a nice little house, Rex knocks on the door. An older man comes to the door.

"May I help you?" he asked in a wiry voice.

"Hi, I am Rex Morgan. I lost contact with Anne and would like to get back in touch with her. Being I'm in town. I hope you can put me in touch with her. I'd like to talk to her and get back to old times if possible."

"Well, she never mentioned you. I don't know, just a minute." Then a woman about the same age came to the door. "Who are you and what do you want?" she asked.

"I am Rex Morgan, I lost contact with your daughter, Anne, and I would like to get back in touch with her, get back to old times if possible. I really enjoyed being with her, she was fun to be with: she said her sister is going to college, studying landscape design. If Anne is here, I'd like to talk to her if possible."

"She's not here; she travels around the country a lot and calls occasionally. If she calls here again I could relay your message if I could know how to get in touch with you or she could."

A young girl came to the door, looking Rex over curiously. "You must be Roxann, the one going to college to study landscape design," Rex said smiling. "Who are you?" she asked.

"I am Rex Morgan, a friend of Anne, I lost contact with her and would like to get in touch with her if possible. If we could meet and have lunch or dinner together again, it would mean so much to me."

Roxann just looked at Rex and smiled. The mother said if Anne called, they would relay the message, and there is no certain time she calls. It could be days before she calls or even a month, the mother said.

"Well, I'll wait for her call then," Rex replied and walked back to the cab, going to the Marriott Hotel to check in and wait. Three days later, the room phone rings. "Hello."

"Hi, how did you find my parents' house?" Anne asked. "Oh, you're a detective, you have ways: you want to meet me and have dinner, why?"

"To be with you, I've missed you terribly."

"You have? Why did you run a check on me and turn me into the police then? You sure have a strange way of showing it."

"First of all, a private detective is an 'official of the court,' that is the way it is and as such, I am required to report anything questionable. It is not a matter of whether I want to or not, I am required to. However, that doesn't change the way I feel about you, I would like to talk to you and be with you. Okay?"

"How am I supposed to believe you?" she asked, suspiciously.

"Meet me someplace so we can talk and have lunch, dinner, or both, look around and if it's safe, then approach me. I'll not make any attempt to approach you. You name the time and place. Okay?"

"I'll think about it." The phone went dead. Two days later, the phone rings again. "Hello."

"You pretending you want to meet me and all the time, two detectives tailing you, you're trying to entrap me," Anne snapped.

"I have two detectives tailing me? That is news to me, I didn't know. I almost was killed twice because of an illegal organization operating under the government's nose. It could be them, they got a picture of me somehow," Rex admitted. "I was the victim of a 'hit and run' going home and the Militia later killed two police officers trying to get me." "I am serious, they almost got me twice, the 'hit, and run,' my car was totaled out, and I was operated on for a concussion and in the hospital for sometime. They have my picture."

"Then you're in the same fix I'm in, they're after me too."

"1 know, but the government can and will protect you. Providing you testify against the Militia," Rex said. "That is what I want to talk to you about as well as see and be with you."

"I don't believe this." she replied. "Is this why you tried to locate me? You want me to surrender and testify?"

"Anne. I wasn't lying when I said I want to be with you. I meant every word of that. Not just surrender, but also give the government the information on the organization. They want to nail them to the wall! They have killed a U.S. Attorney General, an FBI Director, a federal fugitive wanted for questioning, and two police officers protecting me. A lot has happened since you have been gone!"

"How can I believe you, you didn't mention the Militia or investigation the first time we talked. Is this call being traced?"

"Not that I know of, it isn't. This is what I wanted to talk to you about," Rex declared, "and us. The government wants to indict and carry the organization before the grand jury and then to federal trial; they could use your knowledge and I want to be with you."

"Would I receive clemency of all charges?"

"Captain Hilary said all you're wanted for is questioning to see what you know far as he is concerned," Rex replied.

"What about the FBI they have to be included! They would have to give me clemency of all charges as well," Anne stated.

"Let me get in touch with Captain Hilary on that and get him to talk to the FBI, but can I meet and have lunch or dinner, or both with you?" Rex pleaded.

"Get those two detectives off your tail or whoever they are and then maybe," Anne stated stubbornly. "You haven't missed me? You haven't missed me at all." "I have missed you but tailing me and running a check on me, and then putting the police on me doesn't make me feel good about you. How am I supposed to know you're not trying to set me up and entrap me?"

"As I said before, I had no choice, but I am not trying to entrap you or set me up. I am a private detective, not a cop or FBI; set you up or entrapping you is not in my line of work. I can understand how you would feel that way though. I care about you," Rex stated.

"Let me think about it and if I decide to cooperate, I'll call you back. However, get rid of those two 'tails' tailing you or you can forget about me."

"Okay. But if you don't cooperate, the FBI is going to hunt you down, and so is the Militia. I'll contact Captain Hilary to see if he put those two 'tails' on me and about getting you total clemency, the FBI included," Rex stated, agitated that Hilary would put two detectives on him and spook Anne.

"I realize they'll hunt me down, but get me total clemency, the FBI included!" The phone went dead.

Rex called Hilary and asked him if he had two detectives tailing him. Hilary said yes, for your protection; and to see if you would hide Anne. Rex very angry that Hilary didn't trust him, said he was of good mind to hang up. But instead told Hilary about getting in touch with Anne, but only by phone. He told Hilary of her demand of total clemency of all the charges in writing; both the police and the FBI, and the two detectives back off completely! She recognized the detectives; that is probably why we haven't met in person."

"If I do pull the detectives off, who is going to protect you two if the Militia locates you?" Hilary asked, angry that Anne was able to recognize the two detectives. "No problem of the police giving her clemency as long as she testifies, telling everything she knows and did for the organization. But I can't say for the FBI. I'll have to have the Commissioner to contact them and see. We'll have to meet you at the airport and put you both under protection until after the grand jury and the federal trial, then change your identity and everything else about you, and your career."

"You have to get the police and the FBI to give her full clemency of all charges in writing first and full protection, recall your 'detectives' then and only then will she come forward!" stated Rex. "I have no idea where she is, she calls me. If you want her full cooperation, don't tell the FBI, or tell them where we are, if she meets me, we'll be moving anyway! Besides, Anne could probably figure out a way to get us back to Berkeley and be safe as well."

"I'll have to get back with you on the FBI giving her full clemency, either way we'd give you full protection," Hilary said.

"I'd prefer to call you back, and full clemency from both the FBI and the police in writing first, is the only way she will come forward, I have no idea where she is. She has contacted me by phone only. Get those detectives off my back, she recognized them; they're not very good at their job," Rex laughing mockingly.

"Ha-ha!"

Captain Hilary contacts the Police Commissioner who contacts the U. S. Attorney General and explains the situation with the Militia moles in the FBI; and tells of Anne Towers and her demand of full clemency of all charges in writing and full protection in exchange for her testimony.

The U.S. Attorney General, Phil Alterman, says he'll have to check this out and get back to the Commissioner on this, then the message is relayed to Captain Hilary. The two detectives are recalled back their own precinct. Hilary scoffed at them on tailing someone without being recognized. A week later the Attorney General calls the Police Commissioner saying, "She will receive full clemency in writing if and only if she testifies at the grand jury and federal trial, telling everything she knows and did for the organization, giving names and what they did. She will have to tell everything, including what she did and for who, and she has not committed any serious or capital offenses. He would put that in writing, this is faxed to Captain Hilary."

With that cleared up, Captain Hilary waits for Rex to call so he can relay the decision of the U.S. Attorney General. Rex goes out of town to call Hilary, hearing the news and the detectives are recalled and Anne will receive full clemency from the U.S. Attorney General, providing she testifies telling everything, Rex is happy, but nervous at avoiding the Militia. Anne doesn't act overthrilled at testifying but realizes it would put a stop to the government hunting her down and would give her real protection from the Militia of which she now has none. She had not committed any serious or capital offenses, except embezzle the organization, she tells Rex.

"So if we fly back to Berkeley you'll be recognized on sight and we'll both be sitting targets," Anne said. "What do you say I give you a makeover and I have a better idea of getting there safe? We'll discuss it when we meet and eat," avoiding saying whether it would be lunch, dinner or breakfast over the phone. Rex noticed. She is still a smart cookie! "They will be expecting us to fly in instead of what I have in mind being that Hilary said he'd meet us at the airport and you don't tell Hilary any different in case of moles listening in."

"That's an idea, by the time they have figured out we're not coming by plane, we could be half way there or almost there and they wouldn't know where we are," Rex admitted. "The only thing is. Captain Hilary would be wondering where we are. If we're dead or alive."

"Oh well, he'll get over it. If there are any moles in the police precinct, which there might be, we will stand a better chance of surviving by my plan than if we flew as expected and them waiting. If you let your dear 'Captain Hilary' know how we are arriving, someone might be listening in and wait for us as well the detectives. To outwit the Militia, you have to think of these things, think like they think and stay three steps ahead of them."

"I have thought about that, someone in the police precinct but Hilary keeps a tight rein; if there is anybody they haven't had a chance to do anything I'd say, and to cross Hilary is hell!" Rex stated.

"Up to now maybe the two of us together would be too much to resist," Anne replied. At the mention of detectives, Rex told Anne of the detectives staying in his house while he was in the hospital, recovering from the "hit and run" and the two women coming to his house. "Real bright detectives," replied Anne laughing.

The following day, Rex had breakfast in the hotel cafe and then sitting in the lobby reading the local newspaper, was approached by an old-looking woman, bent with age and grey hair asking if he could spare a quarter. Giving her a quarter without bothering to look up, she asked for his newspaper as well, which captured his attention. Looking up he asked, "Anne, is that you?" in a low tone of voice.

"Keep your voice down," she whispered. "Go check out in about twenty seconds, I'll be at the elevators," taking his newspaper and making her way slowly to the elevator, carrying a tan old worn handbag. After she had got to the elevators Rex got up as if slightly disgusted at her taking his newspaper and then walked over to the checkout counter and checking out, pretending to ignore her at the elevator. The two detectives had left sometime before Rex came down to the lobby to go for breakfast.

In Rex's room, he looked at Anne grinning and shaking her head. Laughing, Anne said, "I had you fooled until I took your paper." Rex had to admit he had not recognized her, kissed her, and then packed his luggage while she changed her costume, making herself look like some young schoolchild. She disguised Rex to look like an old man, bent with years of hard work, and aches and pains. Turning in the keys, paying the bill and leaving the hotel, they loaded their luggage into in her car and then go to gas up and eat before starting out on the road. On the road Rex told Anne he didn't have his driver's license back yet and his car totaled had been from the 'hit and run.' They drove a hundred miles before stopping at a roadside rest area. There, Anne put a beard on Rex and gave him a pair of shades and a golfer's cap and sweater. Stopping to gas up and eat, it was another ten hours of driving before entering Oakland County and then Berkeley, Anne feeling very tense and Rex a little nervous as well.

"When we get to the precinct, if I give your arm a slight tug, it means I recognize someone," Anne stated.

"Okay, but you let me know who or which one," Rex replied, nervously.

"I will give you one tug for each person I recognize."

Entering the precinct with Anne's arm in Rex's, casually glancing around, suddenly gave Rex's arm a slight tug.

"The man sitting at the desk to my left and talking on the phone," Anne whispered.

Rex was stunned, Sergeant Oystermen? No, it couldn't be, but Anne whispered he used to be one of the enforcers of the Militia. Oystermen had eyed him at times, but he was always in the company of others and in plain view of everyone else at the different times. Rex didn't know anything about Oystermen or his activities on the outside, it was possible but hard to believe. He seemed to be busy on the phone.

Slowly, Rex and Anne made their way to Captain Hilary's office, closing the door behind them.

"We're here, Captain," Rex announced as Hilary suspiciously watches Rex closing the door behind them.

"I don't believe this," Hilary stammered. "I was wondering what happened to you not coming in at the airport. Why are you in disguise, Rex? I didn't recognize you."

"Anne thought she might recognize (Hilary looks wondering if she's in disguise too) someone from the Militia and she says she does. Sergeant Oystermen. She says he's an enforcer in the Militia."

"Believe it, I recognize him," Anne declared, "Bring him in here and I'll confront him!"

"Okay, but if he is a mole: then I better have my office and this precinct scanned for electronic bugs." Hilary calls for someone to scan his office and the precinct far electronic bugs. Hilary's office and the precinct scanned but finding nothing, Hilary, Rex, and Anne return to Hilary's office. Hilary has a junior officer to come in the office and then called Oystermen's name. Oysterman confused Hilary calling his name, looks around and seeing Rex and Anne still in disguise, is suspicious and wondering. Rex and Anne wait until Oystermen comes in Hilary's office before removing their disguise.

Oystermen walked into Hilary's office, trying to act casual, but fear and confusion showed on his face, which Anne noticed.

"Yes sir?" Oystermen stammers slightly. Rex and Anne remove their costumes. Anne removes her wig as well. Oystermen is shocked at seeing Rex and Anne together. Surprising Hilary as well, actually seeing her in person. So this is the woman Rex has been so fond of, she is pretty.

"Hi Oystermen, remember me, the bookkeeper-accountant? I remember you, although I haven't seen you in about eleven years. Are you still a member and enforcer of the Militias Militia?"

"I don't know what you're talking about, lady, you have me confused with someone else. I don't know you either. I know Rex as many times as he has been in here." He looks stunned which Hilary notices and wonders,

"Oh, I recognize you and I don't forget that easily. What did you do with Jake Willows, the gun smuggler?"

"I don't know anybody by that name and that dirty business, and I don't know you either! You have me confused with someone else!" Oystermen angrily declared, with his voice raised.

"Well, we certainly can find out which of you is lying," Hilary cuts in, moving between Oystermen and the door, which he notices, starting to feel trapped.

"You're going to believe her over me, Captain, as long as I have been here?" Oysterman asked, beginning to sweat and feel panicky.

"You both take the polygraph test," Hilary demands. Rex looking on, studying the faces of both Anne and Osterman to figure out which one is lying, suspecting Osterman.

"I do not believe either one of you until I get to the bottom of this and find out which is lying! What do you think, Rex?"

"Sounds good to me, either that or the 'Truth Serum,' either one will show who is telling the truth," replied Rex.

"I am willing to take either one or both," said Anne smiling. "The 'Truth Serum' will induce a lot of information!"

"Now wait a minute here, I have been eight years doing my job as a detective, I feel that should account for something!" bellows Oysterman, angry and ready to fight.

"What is the matter, Anne has made a serious accusation against you, aren't you willing to take a lie detector test or the 'Truth Serum' to clear your name and prove her wrong? Yes, you have been here for eight years but a charge like this, belonging to an illegal organization under investigation of murder and whatever else, will supersede your service here!" Hilary declared, now suspicious. "She is willing to take both tests but you're not willing? What is the matter? you're sweating!"

"Why did you have to came back or show up here, why couldn't you just remain in hiding and just start over; why?" Oysterman asked in a shaky voice, turning on Anne. She moves back as Rex quickly moves up beside her. The junior detective stares at Oysterman in bewilderment, totally shocked and confused.

"1 got tired of hiding and trying to avoid the Militia and the law too," Anne replied. "It is no fun to constantly be on the run and hiding, not knowing who is after you, the law or the Militia, or both, and becoming paranoid!"

"So, it is true, you're a Militia enforcer?" Hilary asked, looking at Oystermen, still stunned and real disappointed. Rex figured Anne was telling the truth, returning to Berkeley and surrendering to the police, and now seeing Oysterman's face.

"I used to be an enforcer some years ago," he admitted, "but not anymore." The junior detective still stunned just looks at Oysterman, in total shock.

"You were eleven years ago. You might have quit. But I remember you up to eleven years ago," Anne stated. "I didn't see you anymore after that, I didn't know where you went, and in the Militia, you don't ask!"

"If you quit the Militia, why haven't they been after you, and tracking you? You come clean with the District Attorney and they might go easy on you, being you haven't been with the Militia for eleven years and if you haven't committed any real violations or serious crimes, but do not lie! You are not a 'sleeper mole' for the Militia, are you? And what happened to this Jake Willows, the gun smuggler that Anne mentioned?" Hilary quizzed.

"No. I am not a 'sleeper mole' and it's over, except for the Militia, they will come, Anne knows that! Jake Willows, I put him in touch with Barry Williamson. I never saw him after that." With that over Hilary motions for the junior detective to cuff Oysterman: and instructs him to take Oystermen to a holding cell, to wait more questioning from me, the FBI and the District Attorney as well. Handcuffed and baffled. Oystermen is led away, the junior detective still can't believe what he has witnessed and heard, the other detectives looking on and in shock.

"Well, is that it? no more moles here? I hope not! Now, I have the bittersweet job of hiding you two until after the grand jury and federal trial. The District D.A. and the FBI is going to want to question you both, especially you," Hilary said, looking at Anne, curious.

"I will be glad when this is over with and I can get back to a normal life," Anne said.

"Me too," Hilary and Rex replied in unison. "Your questioning hasn't even started yet," Hilary stated. Rex suggested that they stay in the cottage where he had been staying, and tells Anne about it, Anne liked it.

"The Militia knows about that place now," Hilary declared, drawing a groan from Rex and Anne. Hilary tells them about four suspicious characters sneaking onto the property, looking around and looking in the windows of the cottage: carrying assault rifles. A neighbor seeing them calls the sheriff and then the owner, Jason Coatis. By the time the sheriff and his deputies got there, they had left. Jason said you could not stay there anymore: he has put too much money into the place to get it blown away or shot up. How the Militia found about it, I do not know." Hilary admitted; "but someone had to know and tell them. The question is who was it?"

"Well, I can certainly understand that, he has to watch out for his own interest, it is a real nice cottage (Hilary nodding agreeably), you could live there year round. I wouldn't mind having a cottage like that! When the grand jury and federal trial is over, I need to get back to my career. I have worked too hard for too long to get where I am now to give it up," Rex said thoughtfully.

"I couldn't give up not seeing my parents and sister either," Anne declared. "I love them too much, I miss them!"

"Then you had better hope we get them all," Hilary stated. With Anne saying that and coming back to Berkeley to surrender Hilary feels she will tell everything that she remembers, and did. "Otherwise, it is your life at stake! We're going to need to know everything you remember and did, everything you know about the organization. Everything," Hilary stated, looking at Anne. "Where is Kathy that worked at the art gallery and that Oriental looking character, who is he? Where is he?" Hilary asked.

"Kathy, a sweet girl, is living just outside of Oakland with her parents: the Oriental man is Hamil Kasbuil from one of the Mid-Eastern countries; I don't know which country. He wanted me to sell some 'hot' paintings smuggled into this state from somewhere, from where I do not know. I told him that would bring the law down on the gallery and me but he felt I could sell them before you know about it if I played it cool. I knew he would bring more for me to sell, there would be no end to it, and it would be just a matter of time before the law started nosing around and then the Militia!" stated Anne.

"What drew him to you?" Hilary quizzed on.

"He found out I was hiding from the Militia and was using that as leverage to get me to sell his paintings. I do not know where he got them or how, the Militia might have been in on that: and I do not know where he is now or was in the past. I do not care to have any more dealings with him, he is not a nice man by any means, he is mean, vicious, and he enjoys it! He feels no remorse for what he does or to whom he does it!" Hilary listens carefully and takes note of what Anne is saying, he is a dangerous man and extreme caution in approaching him!

"We need Kathy's address, why didn't you notify the police when he approached you about selling his paintings?" Hilary pressed on.

"I suspected the Militia was in this area and they would know where I was and they would have hit me for sure: a mole here and within the FBI proves I was right. I did not want attention drawn to me but, thanks to Rex, I got it anyway. Look how close they came to getting Rex, he told me about the 'hit and run' and the shooting at the

FBI Building, the two real bright 'detectives' staying at his house and the two women coming to the door," Anne replied, laughing. Hilary looks at Rex, embarrassed. Anne then gave Kathy's address to Hilary. Rex standing on the side, listening.

"Well, that is all for now, I may want to question you again, further in detail. Rex coming to have me to do a check on you and your art gallery was only doing what he is 'required under the law.' Being a private detective, he is an officer of the court. You will be grilled intensively at the grand jury and the federal trial with questions," added Hilary. "The FBI will more than likely want to question you too. Before the grand jury."

"I feel like I just got grilled," commented Anne. "The FBI is going to want a go at me too, it figures."

"You have a lot to answer for, you skipped the state when we need to question you, you haven't been exactly straight with us but I now understand why and you have a lot of information; we could start a major investigation. I have only asked a few questions compared to what the grand jury will be asking," stated Hilary.

"I had good reason to not be straight with you, my information is why the Militia wants me dead! We haven't made it to the grand jury yet and look how close they came to getting Rex, they almost killed him twice! If I had stuck around. I would be dead! Can you blame me?!"

"They came close alright, but Rex survived and I think you would have too; we will protect you, both of you are survivors," argued Hilary.

"We will see, I hope we do but I noticed a mole right here in this precinct and I am sure there are some I don't know about, and with bright 'detectives' like Rex told me about (Hilary turning red with embarrassment), we will see," Anne stated, challenging Hilary and giving him a bold stare. Challenging Hilary by a woman was something new to him and most unnerving, something he was not custom to, making him nervous and most uncomfortable. Rex was thoroughly amused!

"Are you through with us for now, if so, where do we go from here?" Anne asked, growing tired of the questioning and Hilary sensing it.

"Good question," Hilary answered, nervous and beginning to sweat.

"How about lunch. I am hungry?" Anne replied. Rex said he was too.

"Okay, I'll take you to lunch and then you come back here until we can find a place for you to stay," Hilary replied.

"Hilary, wherever you put us it is going to have to be a place that the Militia would never think of, to look; someplace most unusual."

"You're right, the Militia will be looking everywhere, it will have to be most unusual to outsmart them," Anne added.

"Do you have any idea where we begin to start looking?" Hilary asked, out of ideas.

"Maybe some little old motel/hotel, nothing fancy as long as it is clean and good cooking, nothing expensive. With Anne's disguises and a place like that we might stand a chance," Rex said.

"Hey. I like that idea but first, I will want to check them out, discreetly. Cheap, nothing fancy but good food, and clean, I like it. It sounds good. Nothing drawing attention. Good thinking," replied Hilary. His spirit brightens a bit.

"What, no shopping malls or nail salon or pool?" Anne teased.

"That is the type of place they will be looking for you; what the Militia will be thinking."

"Are you saying I am high cost maintenance?" Anne continued teasing.

"Oh, you look the part; oh well, let's go eat," Hilary replied. Anne laughing. Leaving Captain Hilary's office, as they passed Sgt. Judy's desk, Judy looks at Anne and Rex, then back at Anne, checking her out. "Is this the mysterious woman, Peggy Lausanne?" she asked, coolly.

"Her name is Anne Towers. Anne, this is Sgt. Judy Sturgis, Captain Hilary's secretary." Rex replied.

"Hi, pleased to meet you," said Anne, smiling.

"Hi, pleased to meet you too," replied Judy. Dryly.

"1 don't think she was happy to see me," Anne said in a low voice after she and Rex had walked away. "Does she have an interest in you?"

"She has been after me to take her out for some time, she is a sweet girl."

"Why didn't you ever take her out?" Anne asked, curious.

"I don't know, no special reason, busy with my cases I guess," confessed Rex. "Are you asking me to take her out?"

"No, just curious, but it's up to you if you take her out," Anne stated.

"You wouldn't be jealous?" Rex inquired, surprised.

"Do I need to be, thinking about it? I guess I would be," admitted Anne, amused. They leave with Hilary to go for lunch, as Judy stands and watch, depressed.

The three of them go to Shellie's Restaurant and Coney Island for lunch and to talk: with Anne telling of her life growing up, her parents and sister, and how she started working for the Militia, Hilary listening to every word. "I was just looking for work back then," she said. Once or twice, Hilary asked a question but he and Rex mainly just listened. Then they returned to the precinct. On entering Judy didn't bother to look up but made herself busy. Rex could tell she was hurt and angry, on the verge of tears, Anne noticed it too.

"You should go ahead and take her out, make a night of it," Anne whispered to Rex after they had moved away past Judy's desk.

"Are you sure you don't mind?"

"Yes, I'm sure," replied Anne.

"But what if she wants to hang onto me and keep me for herself, which I'm sure she will?" Rex replied surprised.

"Then you have a decision to make, which one of us you want. Naturally, I'll be jealous, depressed, and hurt: but she is already deeply hurt," Anne replied softly.

"True, it shows. Okay then."

Later that week, Rex called his friend, Otis Boswell, the club owner and asked if he could issue two evening dinner tickets with no early expiration date for two. Otis said sure, he could do that: it would be a pleasure. "I'm the owner, I can make any arrangements I want for a friend." Rex said he appreciated that and he would be by later to pick them up. Then Rex goes to see Captain Hilary about a car and getting a release on his car and coverage. Hilary said okay, but it might be dangerous with the Militia on his tail. Rex replied that would be a good way to draw the Militia out in the open, and Hilary said, "You got that right," chuckling.

"You and Anne planning on going somewhere, that's pretty risky," Hilary advised, surprised and wondering.

"No, we aren't planning anything but I can't stop living, and I was planning on taking someone else out," slightly nodding toward Sergeant Judy.

"She suggested it. She told me to make an evening of it." Rex whispers surprising Hilary even more and rousing even more suspicion. Was Anne planning to disappear again?

"Well, okay," Hilary replied, suspiciously. Then, Rex whispered about Anne's idea of him and Anne, after Judy and I have already arrived there, to see if she recognizes any Militia moles being I arrive with a date. Anne would of course be in disguise." Rex tells Hilary. "You probably won't recognize her, she is good!"

"Good thinking. Boy, she is a clever one!" Hilary replied, relieved.

Hilary gave Rex a release on his auto, not that its going anywhere in the shape it's in, and Rex calls his insurance and then going to the insurance office, is issued a check to get another car, being the report on the "hit and run" and the paperwork had been taken care of. The doctor had okayed his release to drive. A few days later Rex goes shopping for a new car. He soon settles on a 2005 Cadillac Deville, all power, V-60 engine, 2 door hardtop, and black.

Arriving at Samboa's Rex picks up the two dinner tickets and thanks Otis. The following Monday, Rex stops at the insurance for proof of insurance, then goes back to the dealership for the car, then to the police precinct to show his new car to Hilary and Judy.

"Judy, do you have plans for this evening? If you do, we can make it for another time." Hilary quietly listens discreetly, wondering if Anne has other plans than those mentioned to Rex.

"No, I don't have any plans, why? You and Anne have a quarrel, fight or something?" She asked hopefully with a big smile, Rex asking her out.

"No, I finally got a new car and I want to celebrate, but no, we haven't had a quarrel or fight. She was supposedly a fugitive that I brought in for questioning and we both are targets of the Militia. That pretty much locks us together but I think you knew that," Rex replied. "I thought you did anyway."

"I knew she was wanted for questioning but I didn't know for what and I knew you were a target, but I didn't know she was a target too. Hilary won't tell me anything, maybe it's for the best."

"Believe me, it is. Hilary won't tell you anything in case someone tries to get information out of you. Now. you don't have plans for this evening, you said? I'd like to take you out for dinner if that's okay with you?" Rex asked

"I can't believe this," Judy replied, her face beaming. "What time should I be ready?"

"How does six o'clock sound or is that too early?" Rex asked, smiling. "How does Samboa'sound for dinner?'

"Six would be fine. I'll be ready. I'll be the first woman in your new car?"

Rex said she would be the first woman in his new car, kissed her cheek, said thank you and walked to his car: Judy wondering what happened and brought this about.

"What did I do right to deserve this? if I knew I'd do it again. I have tried and tried to get him to take me out. And now he asks me out," she pondered, her face beaming with laughter and happiness. "Nevertheless, what should I wear to a place like that; it is a high-class restaurant and certainly not cheap!"

At 5:50 p.m. Rex arrived at Judy's house in a reasonable nice suburb and knocks on the door. Almost immediately, Judy answers the door, in a black evening dress, with a low back cutout

"Ah. You look absolutely beautiful, of course you always were beautiful," Rex said and handed Judy a long-stem yellow rose, kissing her on the cheek.

"Thank you, Rex," Judy replied. "I better put it in water, come on in." Judy goes to the kitchen and takes a tall rose vase out of the cupboard, putting water and then the rose in the vase, sitting it on the kitchen table.

"Well. I am ready, I still cannot believe this, you taking me out," she said with a big smile and taking his arm. Rex walks her to his car, opening the dour as she gets in.

On the way to Samboa's, they talked a little about the Militia investigation, without giving Judy any valuable information and then move on to more pleasant conversation, what she did when she gets home and on her days off. Rex told her what he does on his days off and how he pretty much plans what he does on a day-to-day basis.

Arriving at the club restaurant, a bellhop parks Rex's car as he and Judy go into the club for dinner, the band fixing to start warming up and a bellhop takes them to their table with a view of a manicured landscaped pond.

A half hour later, Captain Hilary in a tuxedo with Anne, disguised as a young beautiful lady, of fashion in a real expensive evening gown, arrived, and are ushered to a table across the spacious luxurious dining room. Judy notices Hilary but doesn't recognize Anne.

"Oh, look who Captain Hilary is with? I wonder who she is and where he met her. I would say it needs to be turned around—he is definitely out of her class, he can't afford a woman of her taste and class on his salary," Judy said.

"Well. He must have something going for him, he's with her," Rex replied smiling.

"I don't know what it could be, not with a lady of her class and taste: maybe she's a relative, but still..."

As the patrons started coming in, Anne noticed Rex and Judy. and is impressed with Judy's evening dress.

Suddenly, Anne grasped Hilary's wrist, a signal Rex recognized but did not let on, Anne had recognized somebody, whispering to Captain Hilary. He makes a call on a cell phone and shortly in strolled four plain-clothed officers and Hilary communicates with them by cell phone. Two more plain-clothed officers arrive a couple minutes later. Rex recognizing them wondered how many of the Militia was there. Rex said nothing to Judy, not wanting to spoil the evening and give away Anne. The four plain officers sit at one table and the other two sit at another table three tables away, watching three well-dressed business type men at a table between the officers. As the band starts up, Rex and Judy's meals arrive: stirring Rex's appetite and Judy is ready to eat too. They started eating as they went on talking, Rex stealing a glance at the officers and then recognizing whom they were watching.

Just before the band got into the swing of music and anybody had a chance to get up to dance, the plain-clothed officers moved over to the table of three men, encircling them and quietly announced they were under arrest. The three men seeing that they were outnumbered and surrounded got up and led to the cruisers awaiting them. Judy was surprised, a nice high-class club like this! Otis Boswell noticed the arrest also.

"Well. We've had our entertainment, what is next: did Captain Hilary have anything to do with that arrest?" Judy asked, looking at Hilary and then Rex. "That wouldn't happen to be Anne with Hilary, would it: can she afford expensive clothes and jewelry like that? I certainly can't afford that."

"I wouldn't know, I haven't found out everything there is to know about her yet," replied Rex, looking at Anne and then Judy thinking.

"Then, how do you know if she is being straight about everything and she's not just hoping for protection from the Militia?" Judy inquired.

"How do you know those clothes and jewelry are really hers? 1 wish I could afford that!"

"If she isn't being straight, it will come out sooner or later, if not with the FBI, the grand jury will get it out of her."

"Until then, she has the Militia to deal with, if she lives that long, not that I wish her any harm: you also have them to deal with too."

"She knows that and so do I," replied Rex quietly and thoughtfully. Rex and Judy danced off and on, returning to their table, taking a break after two or three dances. Leaving the club with Judy, Rex drove around seeing the pretty nightlight sights and then up the steep hill he had taken with Anne, overlooking the city with the beautiful nightlights to sit and talk, getting to know each other.

Returning Judy to her house, she said she had a wonderful evening and she could not believe it when Rex asked her out. "This was a setup taking me out so Anne disguised could check the place out, wasn't it?"

"If it was, I still had a great time and I'd like to do it again."

"Who else could it have been? Captain Hilary can't afford women with taste like that on his salary, he is way out of her class," Judy replied with a knowing grin. Rex walked Judy to her door and gave her a good-night kiss.

Returning to where Rex and Anne were staying at a three-star hotel on the edge of town, Rex asked Anne what happened tonight.

"I recognized those three men that showed up at the club as members at Militia meetings and came often to the office building where I worked, sitting in on conferences that I was never included. I was never able to learn their names or what they were to the Militia without raising questions and suspicions about me and why I wanted to know."

"Well. Captain Hilary will get it out of them, if not, the FBI or the grand jury will for sure," Rex replied. Hoping. "Where did you get such nice and expensive clothes and jewelry? Judy said Captain Hilary was definitely way out of his class and he couldn't afford a woman with taste like that on his salary. She didn't recognize you until the end when those

Militia men were arrested. She then realized it was a setup to see if you recognized anybody from the Militia, which you did. She said she couldn't afford that nice and expensive clothes and jewelry like that; she said she still enjoyed it though."

"Good, I am glad she enjoyed the night out. I just hope those three men didn't recognize me though. I could afford to buy these clothes and jewelry when I worked for the Militia; what they paid, I could afford it. They paid me real good! Judy had on a beautiful evening dress, I noticed," Anne exclaimed, with a slight smile.

"Yeah, I suspected she wanted to make a good impression on me, she is pretty, and a man would be lucky to get her" replied Rex.

"Sounds like I have competition, I'll have to watch you more carefully," Anne answered. thoughtfully.

"Oh, you have nothing to worry about, between the two of you. I'll stay with you. You and I have more in common, our tastes, our situation; you're also beautiful and sweet."

"Thank you. I appreciated that last remark, and our situation does lock us together, but I hope I have more going for me than that. If we have to change our style maybe I just might give her my expensive jewelry and clothes?"

"I am sure she would love that!"

"If we have to change our lifestyle, to keep my expensive jewelry and clothes would be awkward; but I didn't say all of my jewelry and clothes, just the expensive stuff."

"You have a point there for sure; I can forget my career too."

The next morning, Captain Hilary said the three Militia men arrested at Samboa's are high officials in the Militia and sponsors as well. Anne suspected that, that was no surprise to her.

"They told you that?" Anne asked, surprised that they said anything at all!

"Yes, threatening to put the word out that they spilled their guts talking. Revealing everything, and then turn them loose on bond, they asked for protection," Hilary replied with a smirk. "That would be putting them out there as targets and they knew it."

"That is a switch. I figured they would clam up for sure, but they probably figured if you turned them loose, the Militia would suspect they talked to be turned loose; and either way they would shoot them for sure to be safe," Rex stated.

Anne agreed. "Loose mouths are expendable."

"All of this 'protection business' is adding up and getting to be expensive," Hilary stated, growing weary and agitated of all the expense.

"Yes, but the funds of the Militia will pay you back and then some," Anne said. "I didn't get it all, they had a reserve that I could not touch, in case of emergencies like now, but I don't know where. I wasn't privileged to that information. I figure it's at some offshore bank or a number of them, maybe the Swiss Bank as well, under fictitious names and accounts."

"I'm of the same opinion," Hilary replied. Rex in agreement as well. "It hopefully will all come out soon in the grand jury hearing and the federal trial," Hilary stated.

"We'll see," Anne replied, hoping Hilary is right. "When is this grand jury hearing supposed to start? I'm ready to get this done and over with, so I can get back to some sort of normal life!"

"When the District D.A. feels confident enough to start, it will begin. It could be anytime soon or be awhile yet, I have no way of knowing when or where offhand. I could ask when, I guess. Arresting these three will most definitely help us a lot," replied Hilary.

"Please ask. I am tired of this hiding and being afraid to show my face in public without disguising myself," declared Anne. Rex said he is tired of it too and ready to get it going also.

"They will let you know. I suspect you will have to give up the money you embezzled from the Militia. More than likely," Hilary said to Anne. Rex as well as Hilary watched for a reaction.

"I suspected that, I used part of it to sponsor the art gallery and the house in Palo Alto. The computers in my house next to Rex's were rental, now returned," Anne replied, casually.

"Where are the paintings now and what were the computers for?" Hilary asked.

"The paintings were in special storage in Luzerne, Switzerland," replied Anne with a slight smile. "They have been returned now: I realized it would be impossible to keep them! They were to be sold on commission: the computers were to keep check on the Militia as much as possible and what was going around me like Rex keeping a check on me," Anne looking at Rex, making him feel a little uncomfortable and ill at ease, he apologized.

"What about the house next to Rex, did you use your own money or embezzled money to get that house?" Hilary asked, continuing to question Anne. "That is a nice house; you and Rex sure have good tastes in houses!"

"I used my own money for that, I wanted to make darn sure the embezzlement money had nothing to do with that house so it would be 'all mine' and mine only with that house!" Anne declared, looking Hilary straight in the eye.

"So, the scheming, hiding, and plotting are all over with now?" asked Hilary; looking back at Anne straight in the eye as well.

"Yes, it is all over with now, including going back to that house," Anne said sadly, looking at Hilary. Rex said, "I really enjoyed my house and will miss that house as well; I enjoyed having a backyard cookout. When I was recovering at my house and we had that big argument, afterward, I fixed a bunch of sandwiches and took a jug of sweetened ice tea to the backyard."

"I am sorry about that and would rather forget that, but you ate a bunch of sandwiches by yourself, you must have put on the pounds. Getting back to 'not being able to return to your house; this will all be behind you and you'll be able to make a new start in life with a clean slate, and a clear conscience. It will be all behind you and over with," stated Hilary.

"Did I really do anything that bad? I don't feel I did anything that bad or wrong! That is cold comfort right now! I'm hoping for a new start, and a new life," Anne wondering if she and Rex can really make a new life together after all that has happened. Rex wondering too. "Will we ever really be free of wondering about the Militia, if they are around or not? I don't think so."

"Maybe not totally free but you will be a great deal more free than now, just a different life-style, name and career," replied Hilary.

"After the grand jury and the federal trial, we'll be free of the grilling and questioning too. I am tired of hearing the grilling and questioning."

"I know you are and I am sorry that I put you through that, but I felt I had to know. Sorry." apologized Hilary. No reply from Rex. Anne looks at Rex then Hilary.

"I am tired of it already too, and Rex has gone through a great deal more than me I suspect," Anne kicked in.

"Captain Hilary felt I was hiding and covering for you, and the FBI suspected that too! But I located you and brought you back," Rex informed Anne. "I have been through the 'gristmill.'" Anne was surprised, grins, almost laughing which Hilary notices.

"This Militia building or headquarters; that you worked at as bookkeeper/accountant, exactly where was it located?" Hilary asked Anne.

"Where I was working. Greenville. Virginia, in the business section of town. I don't think it was the real nerve center of the headquarters, you don't ask a lot of questions without raising suspicion. They had business conferences and meetings there, yes; but I do not think it was the nerve center of the Militia. Wherever it is. I don't know." Anne wrote down the address of where she worked and handed it to Hilary.

"It was just an office building you worked at, that is all you know?" Hilary quizzed.

"Yes the small warehouse section, it was 'authorized personnel only' and they held to that! They had a separate small dock for deliveries and receiving."

"That was it?" Hilary asked, and Anne said yes. "So, what about now. I am here and I pointed out those three at Samboa's do I need a lawyer present for any grilling or questioning at the FBI Building, grand jury and the federal trial? I am feeling I do, you say you have only asked a few questions but I feel it was more than a few! Maybe it was a few in comparison, if so; I would feel better with a lawyer present."

"I think it would be good to have a lawyer present, so you don't get 'something' pinned on you, especially during the FBI grilling, grand jury hearing and the federal trial! It has happened that the grand jury in questioning a witness charged them as well!" stated Rex.

"That is up to you far as a lawyer, I just wanted to know what you know and remember, I have no desire to pin anything on you but I didn't know if we would find you or not; or when and if you would be alive," replied Hilary feeling the heat. "You have a full federal clemency of all charges from the U.S. Attorney General, providing you have not committed any serious criminal or capital offenses. It is my job to question you until I am convinced! You have the FBI and the grand jury and then the federal trial yet! You had better start thinking about the names; and what you did for them, and dates if possible. I feel the grand jury inquiry is going to be very soon now, catching the three characters at Samboa's : plus all the others, and that list of Max Guinean, known as Luke Leprous, had listing names and their activities. I would say the grand jury would more than likely be starting up real soon now! The FBI and District D.A. will want to question you before then to see just what you do know and remember, so they can use it against the suspects in custody," stated Hilary.

"Oh boy, it should be starting real soon then anytime now. Well, at least, it will be over and done with. I hope," said Anne, worried about the grilling and the Militia will be on an all out to get me. Rex is worried about the Militia as well: the rush will be on to shut things down! Hilary seeing Rex and Anne's spirits are low right now, thinking of what is coming up anytime now and the Militia to deal with tries to think of something to lift their spirits. Hilary realizes the Militia will be on a last ditch effort to shut Rex and Anne down.

"It will be rough going through the inquiry and the federal trial, but afterward, it will be over and done with," Hilary stated softly, but it did not seem to help any.

"Yeah, but going through it and the Militia to deal with too," Anne mumbled. "Maybe afterward, we could get away to a place like that cottage Rex was telling about, to recover and relax, unwind?" Rex and Hilary agreed, that would definitely be a retreat!

"When this is over, I am going to need a retreat also: I think I will put in for a long vacation, a month, or so. I haven't had a vacation in a long time; I almost forget what it's like." Rex and Anne urged Hilary to go for it. "You have deserved it!" stated Rex and Anne agreed.

"It would be wise to have an attorney to go with you to the FBI for questioning even if the U.S. Attorney General did give you full clemency," Rex said to Anne. "The attorney would not be able to go with you before the grand jury but he would be outside the jury room if you needed to consult with him. You will more than likely need him during the federal trial to be on the safe side." Anne agreed. "I might need an attorney as well," Rex stated. Anne agreed.

Hilary looking on, surprised at Rex saying that. He asked, "Why would you need an attorney? You brought this case to light and brought Anne back here to Berkeley! You getting an attorney, they might think you have something to hide, I can understand Anne feeling the need for an attorney, but you too, for what?"

"Just to be on the safe side, just in case the FBI or grand jury tries to pin something on me!" Rex declared. Anne agreed with Hilary looking on and shaking his head, amused.

Rex and Anne started to step outside the precinct when Rex noticed a car half block down the street with someone just sitting and watching the precinct. Rex grabbed Anne's arm and pulled her back inside, and told Hilary there is a car half block down the street, with someone just sitting and watching the precinct. Rex had noticed it earlier down there. Someone now knows Rex is here with Anne! Hilary seeing it calls for a deputy on patrol to check it out but by the time he got there, it was gone. Rex and Anne weary of now being watched returned to their motel/hotel room, at Hank inn, on the edge of town. About dusk, a couple of cars slowly approach the courtyard of the inn and then gunning their engines, race through the courtyard with semi-automatics blazing at Rex and Anne's room. Rex and Anne in the back bedroom raise the window, crawl out and then closing the window, flee down the alley to a small cafe. Rex calls Hilary and tells him. Hilary getting the report over the intercom rushed to the motel/hotel and is already there when Rex calls. The Crime Scene Unit arrive within seconds before Captain Hilary and immediately close off the area, then set up their Crime Scene 3-1I Scanner to scan and record the crime scene area. The "first officer" holds the onlookers back. The Crime Scene Specialist take notes of the location of bullet holes, damage to the door of the room, dusting for fingerprints, most possible exit of Rex and Anne out the bedroom window, and what they were doing before fleeing.

"Where are you at, I'll come and get you," replies Hillary, nervous at the thought of Rex and Anne being killed now, with the grand jury so close.

"No, don't come, I don't know how someone found out where we were; it might have been someone watching as we came out but I am wondering if there is someone we don't know about, someone we trust and would never dream possible, like a 'sleeper mole' is watching, listening and reporting everything. Things have happened, coming too close for there not to be! someone is tipping ABC and NBC News as soon as something happens, they may not know the source and then they may but not say anything as long as they get their stories," declared Rex.

"That is scary but you are right about their source, I'm thinking you're probably right about the 'sleeper mole' with what has been happening also, but who and where, here in this precinct? That is scary!"

"Yes, but I feel there is and Anne just now said she feels the same way. Think about it, someone knew about the cottage when you, Jason Coatis, and I were only supposed to know about it. Would Jason actually risk his cottage being shot up if he was the mole?"

"I don't know, maybe if he thought you could be taken alive without shots being fired. I will have to look at him, but I thought 1 had already done that with everybody here. Maybe I didn't look close or hard enough. Being out there by yourselves hiding is very risky but maybe you are safer. Take care and keep in touch," Hilary requested.

Back at the motel/hotel the innkeeper said he called police, hearing gunfire and then seeing six masked men rushing in the room and leaving just before the police got here. The "first officer" took the report; two guest couples staying there didn't see anything or else weren't talking. They heard gunfire, but they were afraid to look out, they were busy going for cover, they said. The motel/hotel owner asked who is going to pay for the damage to that room.

ABC and NBC News are there within minutes to cover the shooting suspecting they will get nothing from Captain Hilary but maybe something from bystanders watching. The "first officer" firmly tells them to stay back of the crime scene yellow tape.

"I understand there was a man and woman staying in the room fired on, it wouldn't happen to be Rex Morgan and Anne Towers, would it?"

"There was a man and woman staying there, but as to who they are I couldn't say, there was no one in the room when I got here. That is all I can say, anything more, I would be guessing. Just stay back of the the line please!" replied the "first officer."

Turning to Captain Hilary, "Captain Hilary, I understand there was a man and woman staying in the room fired on, it wouldn't happen to be Rex Morgan and Anne Towers, would it? Word has got out that she is back in town and that is how you caught those three Militiamen: any comment on that or are you still not talking?" quizzed Jan Roberts persistently, ABC News.

"As I have said before, I have no comment to you two, now or in the near future!"

"Ah, getting nasty again. I must be hitting home," replied Jan with a knowing smile.

"You give me the name of your source and then start helping in this investigation instead of babbling every darn thing, then I will be more responsive to your questions!"

"Captain, we are protected by the California Code, Section 1070, check it out!" declared Harold Jabots, NBC News. Channel 25 News, Fox News, and CNN were there with news cameras as well, taking in everything said.

"I am aware of the California Code, Section 1070! Far as 'hitting home,' if I find out that the Militia is the one tipping you off, and you know the tips are from them or someone associated or the least bit supportive of the Militia and you know it, you two will be on the news! You can count that!" Hilary stated firmly. "Now, I want both of you to move back out of the way and stay out of the way or else you will be arrested! Don't crowd the line!"

"Captain, do you really actually believe we would do that? We do not know who is calling us! We are trying to do our job of reporting the news, we do not mean to hinder or get in the way of the investigation! Believe me on that! Harold Jabots exclaimed. Panicky of where this is leading and the other news reporting channels getting all of this on camera, Harold Jabots is embarrassed and humiliated.

"I do not believe you! Prove to me that you do not know who is tipping you off by finding out who the source is and what his motives are! If you don't, I am going to be taking a look at both of you in 'aiding the enemy and obstructing in a criminal investigation!' Think about that! I would advise you to check on your source and what their motives are, and 'why' they are tipping you!" Hilary lectured sternly.

Jan Roberts and Harold Jabots taken back and alarmed by Captain Hilary's threat, realize they may be in Serious trouble, they are on the threshold of being taken in for some serious questioning, sensing the captain's anger as well seeing it and they are on the news now! Jan is shocked, the table has turned and the focus is on them now, Jan feels a bit of sweat. Stepping back away from the crime scene tape, aware of the other news reporters and news cameras on them, making them feel like suspects, Jan and Harold start to consider this threat from Captain Hilary, sensing they have pushed him too far and now he is ready to turn on them! Jan had heard Captain Hilary is a living nightmare in an interrogation room and she imagined the FBI could be too. Looking at their source in a new light they hadn't considered, they decide they had better see who the tipster is and what his motives are, why he is tipping them. Time in a cell isn't too awful bad if you are used to it, Jan had heard, but she had never been in one! A Militia caller or is it someone sympathetic giving these tips to see if they check out? If it is true, we are definitely being used: we get our stories but at what price! Is it someone from the Militia or someone within the precinct? Captain Hilary has thrown it in their laps to figure out to prove they are innocent.

Captain Hilary going back to the precinct and casually looking around wonders, which one of you is the devilish "sleeper mole?" If I find out, your life is over; you can count on that! A good "sleeper" will bury himself so deep if possible, that it would be pure luck or something happening to draw direct attention to him. Looking and reviewing the files and work records of his staff and officers working in and out of the precinct, nothing stood out, raising alarm.

I guess I should start out by looking first at Jason Coatis again, only closer and further back before he came to work here, and then Jan Roberts and Harold Jabots.

Jason Coatis, a man who enjoyed the outdoors, camping out and hiking. married 15 years with two children, girls 13 and 11. He seemed like a happy family man, always with a smile. His wife, Arlene, an orphan from a foster home, had no bad habits, 40 years old, Jason 45. Jason, also an orphan from the same foster home, they had always stayed in touch with each other. He was an army veteran with four years of service; here in the Vice Squad 4 years. 4 years with the police patrol, he had always taken his job seriously. Looking at his file before he came to work at the police precinct, he went to the Police Academy for two years. Nothing alarming or serious enough to attract deeper internal screening; if not him then who is the mole?

Calling Jason Coatis into his office. Captain Hilary asked, "When I asked about your cottage, did you notice anyone sort of listening in, or did you casually mention Rex staying there to anyone?"

"I can't think of anyone listening at the time, I did mention it to my wife about Rex staying there and she wondered if that was wise with all the news about him and all that has happened."

"Could she have mentioned it to anyone, say to a friend?"

"I don't know, I can ask her, why?"

"Only you. Rex and I, and now you say your wife knew about him staying there, far as I know. Yet the Militia showed up there to grab Rex. I am wondering how they found out, with all that has happened I suspect a 'sleeper mole' somewhere here or loose lips babbling. You have any idea how the Militia found out?"

"Sir, that is scary! I will ask my wife if she told anybody, but I am sure she would never associate with anyone like that or even talk to him or her! I can vouch for her on that, sir! Far as anyone here, Karl Smears at the water cooler looked our way a few times while we were talking."

"You think he could have heard us talking, the water cooler is ten feet away from your desk."

"I don't know about hearing us but I have heard he can read lips, I heard he used to work with the deaf-mute on the side, and they communicate by sign motion and reading lips," giving Hilary a chill. Someone reading lips could read anybody, what they were saying, even in my office with the door closed! This I will have to investigate further! However, there are other possibilities to look at but someone that can read lips wouldn't have to be close by but yet find out anything they wanted by just watching. Here, I thought I had cleared everyone, Hilary felt a bad headache coming on."

Cordell Voletez, a 15-year detective in traffic narcotics, spent one-fourth to half of his time on computer at his desk or on the phone. Cordell's record of his past showed the years before becoming a cop were sort of vague, not much on his family history. His father died from a stroke and his mother had died with lung cancer, his sister had left on vacation, never to return from a cruise or heard from. The investigation on that was a dead end. The cruise Master, Joseph Matroch, said she left the ship, the Fanastic, at Santa Cruz one of the Santa Barbara Islands; there were four witnesses who saw her get off, but did not see her get back on. No one knew where she went; she did not take a cab or rent a car, no one remembers seeing her, but somebody might have given her a ride. There was nothing ever found on board the ship belonging to her. The only driver's license Cordell had been here in Berkeley. His jobs before coming here were odd jobs, nothing stationary or permanent.

Nelsen Bailey, a detective of eight years seemed solid, in the Vice Squad and good at his job. Had been partner with Jason Coatis for a short while, worked uncover after that and now accident investigator. He didn't mind changing around gaining experience in each field. His parents and brother live in Vermont; Nelson felt the need for a change of climate. He was a real estate broker and got to work with a number of different classes of people from all walks of life, he learned to fit in with each one of them. One couple had a yacht and did a lot of traveling.

Bud Eidson, a broker of stocks and bonds, certificates and a collector of rare books and old legal documents from the past centuries: he had some old legal documents that went back three centuries. He is now in the illegal gambling, scheming and sham operations unit, and 19 years. His father has cancer and is in a home: his mother was accidently killed by a drunk driver, in Maryland. His sister supervises a small chain of jewelry stores: and keeps a check on the father; his brother in Texas worked in the oil industry as a crew supervisor.

These four detectives seemed solid good detectives and good at their jobs. Hilary knew he could call in Internal Affairs to check out the precinct but he wanted to give a try first, it would look better for him if he discovered the sleeper mole in his own precinct; if things don't get too hot. His staff knew if they were into anything like the Militia and Captain Hilary found out, it would be a sad day for them! Nevertheless, someone had gotten word out about the cottage and Hilary felt sure it almost had to be from this precinct or someone connected to it!

1 need to find a way to draw them out in the open, show himself or to lead to him, Hilary felt. See if Rex or Anne has any ideas when they call. Shortly thereafter, Rex calls to see if Hilary had come up with any idea how they were tracked down and Hilary relays conversation with Jason Coatis and the need to draw out the sleeper in the open. Rex telling Anne of Hilary's idea of drawing out the mole, Anne suggests having a birthday party or anniversary party with the staff only. We would have to keep our eyes and ears tuned to anything suspicious, anything that doesn't feel or look right. Hilary said that is a good idea but risky. That seems the only thing to do right now, but who is to be the "bait," Hilary asked. Anne said she has a birthday coming up in a month, which should draw out the mole. That would be like honey drawing bees; she would be the "bait" as long as she has protection.

Anne saying she would be the bait, a birthday party for her at Rex's house, decorations all inside only with only the staff to know one day before the party. Meanwhile, Rex and Anne stayed at a low rundown hotel and ate at the small, cheap fourth class cafe, sensing the Militia would never think of checking some place like that. The day of the party, the staff arrives at Rex's house, Captain Hilary, Rex and Anne already there and watching as everybody including Sgt. Judy coming in, brings their gift. Everybody looks at Anne, "So, this is the woman the news has been all about?" Over at a table set up for the gifts, with a forensic scanner attached beneath to scan and detect a bomb, explosive or lethal chemicals.

Sure enough, a package is set down very carefully and the tiny red light underneath starts blinking. The detective, Karl Smears, sitting it down carefully, starts to join the other detectives, but Captain Hilary, Rex and Anne seeing the blinking red light, quickly move up to hold him at the table.

"You open it, Karl," Anne requests.

"No, you are apparently the birthday girl, you open it."

"No, you open it!" snaps Captain Hilary.

"It's not my birthday, it's hers, let her open it," replies Karl suspecting he has been trapped; this was a setup. "Please sir, I would rather not," Karl pleads.

"Why? What is in there that you would rather not open it?" barks Captain Hilary. The other detectives looking on, are stunned, now realizing this was not just a birthday party for Anne, but more of a trap to snare a sleeper cell.

"A powdery type of toxic vapor boron, mixed with sulfuric acid, pressurized in a makeup kit."

"So, when Anne opens it, it blows in her face! You are the 'sleeper mole.' You are under arrest. Karl Smears!" With that, Hilary calls the two officers from the bedroom to take him away. Forensics takes Karl's "gift" as evidence. "Save us a piece of that cake!" the officers requested.

"Well, that is over, I don't know if I feel up to celebrating now or not," stated Anne.

Rex says, "I have survived two attempts on my life but I am still here. All of these presents and food, at least let's eat!" The detectives are all for that, they are hungry after this little plot. Everybody grabs a plate and digs in, afterward, Anne cuts the cake, and they consume that. Then Anne opens the gifts; some of the officers and detectives asked for the autograph of "The mysterious woman making the national news headlines."

Back at the precinct. Captain Hilary questioning Karl Smears intensively, Karl confessed he is the one informing ABC and NBC News, the Militia watches the news for the information. He informed the Militia about Rex staying at Jason Coatis's cottage also. "Why?" demands Captain Hilary. Karl claimed the Militia said they are aware of his mother in an assisted-living home. "Sheila's Place" Care Home and they know where I live, my beautiful wife, Natalia and my two lovely daughters, Katina and Kalai, going to Berkeley Junior High. To make their point, Katina came home and said, some man said to tell Karl he has two lovely daughters. They know where Natalia gets her hair done, where I go to get a haircut, where she goes shopping and our favorite place to eat. Nellie's. They know our daily schedule; they know also everything about my family and me!

"Well, I can understand why you did what you did, but you should have come to me. You have broken the law, the D.A. might go easy on you under the circumstances, if you cooperate and tell everything. Did they approach you in any way other than your daughter?"

"Katina brought home a sealed envelope stuffed in her school backpack, addressed to me; my wife opened it and called me home to read it. Just what could you have done if I hadn't went along? My family's life is at stake! Katina didn't see who stuffed it in her backpack; she found it after she got home!"

"Your family will be moved to a federal safehouse and be under federal protection. As for you that is for the D.A. to deal with; I have nothing to do with that, which is beyond my jurisdiction. You babbling about Rex going to the FBI Building for questioning got two police officers killed; that is a serious offense. "

"Like Rex and Anne, they came close to getting them, I came close to getting Anne and Rex has had two real close attempts on him! Being that I am now out of the picture, there will be someone else, probably forced to go along with their family's life at stake like I was!"

"What do I do?" wondered Hilary. Talking to Rex and Anne, they said the police or FBI needs a mole inside the Militia, give them a taste of their own medicine; "If that is possible?" stated Anne, "The Militia keeps a close watch for stuff like that, I sensed that while working for them! If the mole was caught, they would deal with him quite different than you do. I certainly wouldn't want to be her."

"In that case, what 'sucker' do we use for a mole and how do we get him in?" asked Hilary.

"Create a really bad character who hates the government and he will have to commit a few crimes and even kill a cop to get the Militia to even notice him, much less consider him and maybe let him in. Even then, he would be on a 'trial basis' to see if he is for real and his life would be stake if he fumbled or raised the slightest suspicion," stated Anne.

"Who would volunteer for something like that, it would have to be somebody with no family, and definitely no ties or connections to anyone like friends," stated Hilary,

"Use one of the suspects you caught, if you can trust them, not yet missed and word hasn't got out yet!" replied Rex.

"The ones caught so far have been locked up long enough to be missed and I suspect word has got out as well. The only one not missed yet is Karl Smears, but if his family were to quietly move, and quickly disappear the Militia more than likely would suspect something and investigate why. That would fix Karl for sure as a mole," stated Hilary.

"The only choice then, to get someone who enjoys taking high risks, playing 'cloak and dagger' to volunteer if there is someone willing, but be prepared to offer a huge retirement if they succeed and survive," replied Rex. "Good luck on that!"

"Thanks!" groaned Hilary, Rex and Anne laughed. "I had better take this to the Commissioner, let him handle it and decide what to do."

With that said, Hilary decides this is his way out of this fix, take it to the Commissioner to decide and lift the burden off his shoulders. Hilary feels like Rex, good luck on finding someone brave enough and who likes taking life-threatening risks to become a mole, and this is for the FBI to handle, let the Commissioner call and talk to the FBI. With the recorded confession of Karl Smears and his statement of his family at risk, plus Rex and Anne's suggestion about the FBI placing a mole within the Militia, Hilary goes to see the Commissioner, Wayne Melton, and lays it out to him.

"Anne Towers says the Militia really watches for moles and snitches, she sensed that when she worked for them, she says the FBI's mole's life will be a high life-threatening risk!"

"The mole surely would be made aware of that. I will call the FBI and tell them about Karl Smears, and his need for protection for himself and his family, being that he confessed. I will also suggest like Rex and Anne said, slip a mole inside the Militia if they don't already have one. Someone willing and likes taking high risks would probably be someone single and no family or friends, hopefully, whomever that would be! We could keep Karl where he is and he feed the Militia false information but his family would get it in the neck. If we hide them, the Militia will suspect something gone sour and Karl will become a target."

"How about feeding ABC and NBC News a few false stories to trace and see what happens? We will have to keep a watch on Karl's family for certain then, if not now!" suggested Hilary.

"If the Militia sense that the Smears' family is being guarded, they will suspect something, the family could get it for sure then, from a long range sniper. In addition, maybe the wife shot by a sniper while shopping or getting her hair done; or the daughters fail to come home from school, or both? I will talk to the FBI; they have a new director now. Milton Bradley. He is a real tough one, goes by the book like the Internal Affairs Director, Larry Flippant! They call him, the Head Hunter."

"That should take care of the moles in the FBI then. I will wait for your call, where do we put Karl Smears and his family?" Hilary asked feeling relieved of making a decision.

"I will get back with you on that, keep him under 'protective custody' for now, we'll see if his family and him can be moved today, the FBI will want to question him for sure," stated Melton.

"He knows that and he is willing, he is concerned about the safety of his family, more so than his own."

"The FBI wants to question Anne Towers before she goes before the grand jury inquiry to see what she knows and remembers so they can be prepared to question the Militia suspects. I understand Rex Morgan only knows about Anne Towers known as Peggy Lausanne, nothing more. Is that correct?"

"He says that is all he knows and remembers, I have grilled him good on that, he described the Oriental character and looked at the mug shot files but did not see him, a fax of him has been sent to the FBI and Interpol, they didn't have anything. Anne Towers knows she is to be questioned by the FBI and the grand jury, and she is prepared but feels the need for an attorney in case the FBI or the grand jury tries to 'pin something' on her," stated Hilary.

"She feels they would do that? Well, the grand jury has occasionally charged the witness, but only if they feel there is sufficient and probable cause," acknowledged the Commissioner.

"She says she wants to get this over with so she can get her life back and she can't give up seeing her parents and her sister. She has high regard for them."

"If she goes into 'witness protection' seeing her family could be risky for them as well as for her. I suppose she knows that?"

"She does, but she wants to get this over." stated Hilary. "Don't we all," replied Commissioner Melton.

"Does the FBI have enough evidence on the Militia to go to the grand jury and for a federal trial?" asked Hilary.

"They say with what they have gathered up, Anne Towers tells what she knows and with the Militia suspects opening up in the grand jury inquiry, they feel they are ready. But they want to question Anne Towers first."

"If the Militia's attorneys don't find some loophole or cause to squash the suspects' and Anne's testimony, or delay the hearing."

"The FBI says they are prepared for that, they are expecting the Militia to try something like that."

"As Anne says, 'we will see,'" replied Hilary, worried that it may fall apart over some loophole or cause, or both. "I'm sounding like Rex and Anne now, but they expect the Militia to try something, in court or outside of court."

"Hope for the best but prepare for the worse."

"Have the FBI set a date to question Anne Towers and I will try to make sure she is ready," replied Hilary. "An attorney will be with her. I think she is firm on that."

"Okay. I will relay that to Milton Bradley" replied the Commissioner. "Has she picked an attorney yet?"

"No, but I am sure he will be a darn good one, she doesn't leave anything to chance!"

Commissioner Wayne Melton calls the FBI Director Milton Bradely to discuss Rex Morgan and Anne Tower's idea of placing a mole inside the Militia and get a date set for questioning Anne. She says she wants an attorney to be with her in case you or the grand jury try to pin something on her and Rex Morgan agrees with her. The FBI Director laughs; then says to not let it go any further than Captain Hilary but there is already a mole inside the Militia but it's most difficult to communicate with him without blowing his cover. The undercover mole suspects there are leaks or loose lips somewhere but he has not found out where. The FBI Director looking at his schedule/calendar suggests in a week at 10:00 a.m. A date has been set for the grand jury to begin, two months at 9:00 a.m. From there, the federal trial will shortly thereafter begin. Wayne Melton makes note of it on his schedule/calendar and then calls Captain Hilary to inform him. "About the 'mole,' there is already one inside the Militia but it is to go no further than you; that is the FBI Director's order!" stated Commissioner Melton.

"You feel I am holding back?"

"I feel you have told everything about yourself and your past and I hope you have, but I only know you from when you moved in next door to me: I know nothing about you before that other than what you have said." Anne just looked at Rex. "I am for you, Anne: I care about you, really,"

Anne just walked to the window, looking out, saying nothing. Rex doesn't know whether to go to her or not, but goes to her, anyway, hugging her. Anne turns and buries her face against his chest, clinging to him.

"Right now. I just need you to hold me."

Rex doesn't know whether to suggest Hilary and the FBI look into Anne's background or not, being an officer of the court: if he suspects something, he is supposed to report or mention it to the police. However, it is just a hunch, nothing more to go on or to back up the hunch. Therefore, he is not required to report it; besides, I care for Anne. Nevertheless, the feeling continues to linger that she might be holding something back and concealing her past, making Rex most uncomfortable. Rex says nothing more to Anne about her past but decides to wait and see if she comes forth, either to him, Captain Hilary or the FBI. Anne stressed, goes around the apartment as if she has something on her mind and something is bothering her. Rex says nothing but senses that she is under great stress. The nickname of the new FBI Director and him earning it worries Anne.

Three days before she is supposed to go for questioning by the FBI Director Anne nervously asks Rex what if she had not completely revealed her past, what would happen to her?

"I would say it depends on the seriousness of it, if you own up to it to Captain Hilary now, he will grill you or pass it on to the FBI or both.

As for the FBI. I cannot say. It all depends on the seriousness of what you did or didn't do," Rex replied. "I would suggest you talk to the captain. telling him everything from your past, leaving absolutely nothing out."

"I blackmailed a CEO who cheated on his wife and defraud the company of $70,000 to buy a cottage so he and his lovely mistress could go there on weekends occasionally. I sent pictures of him and the mistress together in public and them at his cottage, but no direct contact. I had him to transfer the money to an account set up for that purpose; then I withdrew the money and closed the account. He couldn't file charges without exposing his fraud," stated Anne. "This happened ten years ago."

Hearing this, Rex is disappointed and saddened, knowing he must report this to Captain Hilary and he in turn will tell the Commissioner, who will tell the FBI. This will more than likely break Anne's clemency and she might be charged but to get her testimony, they might drop it or give her a light sentence and full protection. I must report this to Captain Hilary and let him handle it from there, Rex tells Anne. After the confession over the phone, Captain Hilary says she must come in and put this in writing and being that she held this back, a thorough background check and there would have to be an inquiry on her to make sure there is nothing else she is holding back. Rex and Anne arrive at the precinct, both knowing she is in for a stern rebuke from Captain Hilary. Hilary asked if she wants an attorney present for questioning, Anne says no, she knows she has this coming, not confessing everything from her past. "Who likes to confess and admit how bad they have been? It is not a good feeling!"

Hilary agrees, "but in an investigation, it must be done." Anne puts her confession in writing at Hilary's request.

"You told me you embezzling the Militias Militia organization was it, that was all you did, and now you own up to this! The FBI Director, Milton Bradley will grill you well!" Hilary declared, really agitated that Anne would withhold this information and not come clean. "I will let Bradley decide if you have confessed to everything or not, as for your clemency, I cannot say now, it probably is up to the District D.A. Being that the U.S. Attorney General gave you full clemency, providing you tell everything, it might be up to him. I don't know how he will feel about this! It would have been better for you if you had owned up to this in the beginning!"

Anne Towers stressed and drained, sits down to await the outcome of her predicament. Hilary goes over to a female detective and tells her to "keep your eye on Anne Towers, not to let her out of your sight and don't let her leave!" Hilary calls the Commissioner and gives him the news on Anne Tower's confession just now, and statement in writing.

"This is a fine time to find this out, three days before she is to be questioned by the FBI Director, he will love hearing this!" stormed the Commissioner Wayne Melton, sourly. "I will pass it along to him, try to get as much out of her as you can to see if there is anything else she is holding back! Also, fingerprint her and get her mug shot, then run it through the FBI files and Interpol to see if anything comes up! Keep her there until I hear from Milton Bradley himself!"

"She is really depressed right now, I'll hold her and wait awhile before starting in on her," replied Hilary. "Good, she should be depressed at withholding this information! She might be facing a number of charges!"

"I will let you rest and relax a bit but I have to question you to see if there is anything else you're holding back. I have to have you fingerprinted and get your picture taken and run it, which came straight from the Commissioner!" Hilary tells Anne. "If you are hungry, I'll send for something; if you are, you might feel better." Hilary ordered a bunch of sandwiches, chips and pop for Rex and Anne. After they have finished eating, Anne fingerprinted and her picture taken: front and both right and left sides, this to be run through the FBI and Interpol while Anne is being questioned. The female detective leads Anne is to an interview room, for questioning by Hilary and Rex to observe. Hilary turns on a tape recorder, asked if she wants an attorney to be present and Anne said no. The questioning by Captain Hilary goes for a good three hours, Hilary grilling her good, everything recorded. It was almost more than Rex could take, Hilary grilling Anne as if she was a cold-hearted felonious suspect, but Rex knew he could not interfere: that would not set well with Hilary. Hilary has to question Anne for not revealing all of her past. During the grilling Anne broke down weeping, and at the end as well; broken and depressed, completely drained, Anne looked at Rex as if he should have helped her but realized he could not, she was on her own in this. This brought back memories of his questioning.

"I will turn this confession and handwritten statement over to the commissioner and he will most likely pass it along to the FBI Director Milton Bradley or maybe the D.A. to decide if your clemency still stands or not. I can't say," stated Captain Hilary. "You will have to stay here for now until I find out where you stand. We will still need your testimony on the Militia and you will still be under the federal witness protection, regardless you withholding until now. You have that in your favor. The Militia defense will probably use this to play down the effectiveness of your testimony. They are entitled to this disclosure in 'Discovery.'" Rex and Hilary realize that she will more than likely still demand full clemency for her testimony.

Rex realizes Anne is not the sweet innocent woman he thought she was; I will have to regard her with the utmost caution now until she proves herself far as her tendentious behavior. Do I still want to live and be with her, wondering what is on her mind; can I fully trust her? Rex ponders. This I have to think about. Anne senses that Rex is taking all of this in and thinking about their relationship in a new light now. We are stuck together for now. Anne is hungry again going through this hellish nightmare and Rex is hungry having to listen to this and remember what he went through. Hilary says he will have to order and have it delivered, in light of Anne's present predicament.

Three hours later, the Commissioner calls to see if the captain has come up with anything from the FBI files and Interpol. "Not yet," replied Hilary. The Commissioner said Milton Bradley is checking the FBI files and Interpol himself, and has not decided on Anne's situation, he has forwarded it to the D.A. and contacted the Attorney General's office. He wasn't in but a message will be delivered to him. The Director realizes we still need her testimony and may have to continue her clemency and witness protection to get it. However, without the clemency, she could face blackmailing, conspiracy to commit blackmail, using a bank and running a criminal enterprise; which could rack up a long term prison sentence. Bradley figures the Militia's defense will use this to weaken her testimony's effectiveness if they find out or hear about it. We aren't forced to show it to the defense but it has to be available to them through Discovery. Do not say anything to her just yet, let her sweat it.

"She is really depressed. I grilled her good, she broke down during the questioning and at the end; and she was hungry again, Rex also. I think it was almost too much for him, he just observed," stated Hilary.

"He must care for her then."

"Yeah, but I think he saw her in a new light, he hasn't said anything, sort of quiet like he's thinking."

"Maybe he is. I could certainly understand why!"

Jan Roberts from ABC News called to say she and Harold Jabots of NBC News have not received any more calls or tips from the mysterious tipster tipping them to any news. "Have you found who he is and arrested him?" Jan asked.

"What makes you think or ask that? That was your job to find out who he is! Maybe, the reason he has not called is that there is not really anything to report. It is your job to find who he is; I still wonder about you two if you are the sympathizers of the Militia, I still suspect you two! You prove me wrong by passing along some useful information to help out in the investigation!" strongly advised Captain Hilary.

"Here we go again, we are not Militia sympathizers, we are news reporters just doing our job!" stormed Jan. With that, the line went dead.

That should put an end to them, thought Hilary, smiling. Like a flash, the thought came to Hilary, if they want to help, let them run the Oriental character's face and name, Hamil Kasbuil on the news to see if anyone recognizes him and knows where he is! Hilary calls Jan Roberts back.

"This is Captain Hilary; if you want to help out in the investigation how about running an Oriental character's face and name on the news to see if anyone recognizes him or knows where he is? We haven't found anything on him and haven't been able to trace him, it's like he disappeared."

"Ah, you need us to help you, okay, to prove we are not with the Militia, we'll do it. Give me his name and you will need to fax his picture to me and to Harold Jabots also. Give me his name."

"Hamil Kasbuil is his name according to Anne Towers. She says he is a mean vicious man, he feels no remorse for what he does or to whom. According to Rex Morgan, he is medium height, stocky built, and has a confident expression. He is an Oriental nationality: Anne doesn't know what country he is from."

"Sounds like a real nice friendly person to know," replied Jan sourly. "I hope I don't meet him!"

"If you see or meet him, call me as soon as possible, we need to talk to him, and get him off the street."

"I hear you there!" replied Jan. Hilary faxed the face and name of Hamil Kasbuil, then contacts Harold Jabots to get him to run Hamil's picture and name as well. "Would it be possible to do an interview of Anne Towers in person?"

"Not right now, she is in hiding until after the grand jury and federal trial. Maybe after that, but do not announce that she is hiding, the Militia probably already knows that, but I don't want to confirm it."

"I will run it in the evening news, thank you for calling. If you have anything more, call Jan and I. we'll run them on the news! If you catch him, can we have a news report on him?"

"I will give you as much as I can without blowing our investigation, I might be able to give you more later on."

Within a few minutes, the Commissioner calls Hilary.

"The FBI Director didn't see or find anything far as the FBI files or the Interpol; they had nothing on Anne Towers. Either she hasn't done anything to draw attention to herself or else she has concealed her past really well. Milton Bradley is now consulting with the U.S. Attorney General about her concealing her past until now being he gave her full immunity," stated Wayne Melton. "Keep her there until I hear from Milton Bradley on what the Attorney General says." Hilary tells the Commissioner about faxing the Oriental character's picture and name to Jan Roberts from ABC and Harold Jabots from NBC to run on the evening news. The Commissioner said, "You might find out something, somebody might have seen him or know where he is if the Militia don't execute him."

"Okay, will do," to keeping Anne at the precinct until the Attorney General makes a decision. The next day, the Commissioner calls again to relay the U.S. Attorney General's decision.

"The Attorney General feels we have no choice to but to continue giving her immunity and witness protection for her testimony providing she has been truthful and forthcoming and this time there is nothing else being held back or being kept secret. However, if she is still concealing anything else, then she can and will be held for obstructing and concealing. Her testimony would be tarnished and ineffective if she is still withholding, if it isn't already. To keep this immunity and full protection, her testimony must be convincing and effective! Relay that to her; make darn sure she understands the seriousness and the consequence of it!"

"Okay, I will lay it out to her," stated Hilary. With that, Hilary returns to Anne and Rex in the interview room to lay out the decision of the U.S. Attorney General and the penalty of concealing anything else, regardless how small. Anne says she understands. Hilary and Rex wonder about that. "Also, your testimony must be convincing and effective! That came from the U.S Attorney General himself'

"It's just that! I was afraid of what might happen if I admitted both the embezzlement and the blackmail as well. But it was bad people that I used, if that counts for anything," Anne stated.

"Yes, you used bad people but that doesn't excuse what you did! It is still a crime! If you hadn't come forward and admitted this, after you gave your testimony and then we found out, you would have been charged. However, knowing about it now, as you stated on tape and in writing, we could not charge you for it later. However, if you are still withholding and it is found out, your testimony would be tarnished and ineffective; and you could and would be charged!"

"I am not concealing anything else."

"That is what you said earlier, we will see if you are or not! We will see, believe me on that!" Anne sits there feeling like a convicted felon, Rex looking on, silently, depressed. Anne shamed and humiliated doesn't look at Rex.

Silently. Rex and Anne return to their apartment to wait the day of Anne going for questioning by the FBI Director. Round two of intense grilling coming up, Anne feels, but the attorney will be with her.

"You'd best be thinking about what attorney you're going to use. I don't think it would be good to go for the FBI questioning without an attorney present, especially now," stated Rex.

"Yeah, I know. There is an attorney in Charleston I think would be good or knows someone who is good," replied Anne.

"I suspect you are going to need someone better than 'good'; he needs to be sharp and witty, someone who is known as a sharp lawyer, knows the law inside and out. I understand Milton Bradley is 'old school'. Hard nose, crafty and sharp too!"

"You think I'm still withholding something?" Anne asked, concerned that Rex thinks she's not capable of telling the truth and totally revealing her past. "It's hard to admit something like this, I'm not proud of this."

"Yes, I suppose it is, but I thought you laid it all out when you told about embezzling the Militia organization and now you admit this blackmail. Breaking down during the questioning and at the end, I feel maybe this time you told it all but I don't know. I knew you as Peggy Lausanne until I found out different."

"I am sorry. I need to prove myself but you feel I need someone sharp and witty in case I'm still withholding something?" asked Anne, "This next time. I could be charged big time; I'm not willing to risk that."

"No, not necessary that but in case the Director tries to 'pin something' on you to make sure you are locked in as a real 'shady witness' to continue suspecting and questioning you later."

"I see your point, you are right." Anne contacts the attorney in Charleston and tells him somewhat of her situation. "I need a sharp attorney, someone knowing the law inside and out, and better than good!"

"I know a lawyer in Oakland, close to Berkeley but he is expensive! He charges $200.00 an hour plus expenses." Anne takes his name and phone number, makes an appointment for consolation, free if he takes the case. To take the case, he requires $500.00 upfront to start, above the hourly fee. The reputation of Andre' Knowles' reputation in the "white collar" business circle, as a highly successful lawyer, seldom loses a case.

"You have money for a lawyer like him?" Rex asked, curious. "You will need him during the grand jury inquiry and the federal trial as well, you should remember that."

"Yes, I know but he is good! I have the money when I need it," Anne replied.

Cheryl Nickles, the Assistant District Attorney, playing on a hunch, shows Barry Williamson pictures of Militia members to see if he recognizes or knows anything on them. Barry starts looking casually but comes to a stop looking at one, laying it down nervously.

"Who is he, why are you so nervous?" Cheryl asked, anxiously.

"Because he is referred to as 'Mister,' I do not know his name or anything about him except you have to be in 'inner circle' to know him; but I have heard he is bad news to cross , with big connections. (Cheryl picks up his picture looking at it.) He has a lot of influence with big wheels of corporations, government officials and rumor has it, with congressional representatives too. I am in the group below them," Barry replied. "If I were you, I would want some man with me in a room with him."

"Thanks for the warning. Cheryl still looking at the picture. What about these others, where do they fit in; and who are they to the organization; how much weight do they carry?"

"They are sponsors, advisors, and recruiters to bring in the 'big fish' like corporation CEOs, congress representatives, and a few certain government officials that could help the Militia."

"Oh I see. Well, we need a list of the CEOs, certain government officials and congress representatives," Cheryl replied. "We need you to point out which of these men are sponsors, which are advisors, and which are recruiters also." Barry looks at Cheryl as if she felt he could perform miracles.

"That is a tall order, some of them I only knew vaguely!"

"You can take your time figuring out who are who and what, but we need to know in presenting it to the grand jury and for the federal trial. We get these suspects put away will make it easier to protect you."

"They will cover up and hide their role in the Militia. You realize that, don't you?"

"Yes. I realize that, we will have to prove their roles and make them face up to it."

"It's easier said than done with these characters!" Barry replied.

"We shall see," replied Cheryl feeling challenged and wondering if he is right. Cheryl leaves the pictures with Barry to work out who is who and what role they play in the Militia.

"I never dreamed that I would end up in a fixed situation like this," stated Anne to Rex. "I figured on owning a business like the art gallery and I would have if you had not caught onto me, meddling, and messing it up for me."

"I am really sorry about that, I really mean that, but being an official of the court I was required to go to Captain Hilary with this. I never dreamed that I would end up in this situation either. I can forget about my career as a private detective, that is history now. It was a real good profitable business and a real good income for me, I could afford the house and lifestyle I had and the future looked good for me. I started out as a kid building up for this career but all of that is history now. I have to start over from scratch now," stated Rex. "I wish I could have minded my own business, stuck to my cases and kept on working."

"Me too, I have to start over as well. When I was a little girl, I used to wonder what I would grow up to be and what my career would be like. I used to dream and fantasize different careers I would like. My mother would say, 'first, I should enjoy being a child and having fun, not be anxious to grow up, that would come soon enough.' But I always wondered what I would be," replied Anne.

"I used to play 'cops and robbers.' I would sit around reading detective stories and watching detective and FBI movies on TV. My parents bought me a computer for Christmas one year to do my research on the detectives, FBI, and the CIA. Even as a child growing up, the pattern was pretty much set for my future career, I never deterred from the 'cops and robbers' or detective mode from a child on up, never thought of anything else for a lifetime career," Rex continued.

"Where are your parents now?" asked Anne, curious.

They are in an assisted-living home now, their health failing them, I need to go see them as soon as possible, let them know I have not forgot them. My career just kept me so busy I haven't had time to go see them for the past three years," Rex replied, feeling guilty.

The FBI Director calls the Commissioner to tell him, the Militia has brought in an outside sniper, a real crack shot; rumor has it that he is an exceptional sharp shooter. Once he gets the target in the "crosshairs," they are good as dead. He is to take out Anne and Rex too, if he gets in the way. He is to take out the inner circle of the Militia members also, if they show their face in public. They learned that Rex is not a threat, he only knows Anne as Peggy and that he knows nothing more than that.

This information passed on to Captain Hilary, causing him to feel nervous. Rex calling Hilary, he tells Rex the news, causing Rex to feel tensed and nervous, Rex tells Anne and she becomes panicky but is not surprised.

Cheryl Nickles. The Assistant District Attorney, the Militia Celebrities, learned that the Militia organization is interlocked together by each organization having executives on each other's broad of directors with decision making options and with voting privileges, sort of like a web. One broad executive is the owner PIETA & Associates, a law firm: there are no names given as to the executives on the broad of directors. None of them actually knew where the ringleader lived or stayed, one thought he might he somewhere in Brazil, Argentina or Peru but was not sure. No one had seen him and lived; he has not allowed anyone to photograph him for 30 years. He always had a variety of names and disguises for traveling so no one would recognize him or know his true name or identity, very reclusive and craved privacy. So who would know when he entered the U.S.? Seize someone close to him but how would they know that? Find some way to force him to identify himself, but how would they know it was really him or someone else? Shut the corporations down and freeze their assets: but what about their "unknown" assets in foreign banks and vaults. Let the District Attorney, the U.S. Justice Department, and the U.S. Attorney General figure that out, Cheryl Nickles decided. All I have to do is get these characters ready for the grand jury and the federal trial.

Anne Towers, realizing the FBI would want a list of names and possible dates, as close as possible, mentioned in the bookkeeping and accounting, sat down to list names and dates as best as she could remember. Anne makes a list for herself as well, to keep in case she should need it. U.S. Congressional Representatives and State Congressional Representatives were in the list, which would bring uproar, national and state. There would be impeachments handed out, some scrambling for cover, and some resignations, both national and state. Anne contacts her attorney, Andre' Knowles' office to make sure he's still on board to go with her to the FBI headquarters for questioning the day after tomorrow, at 9:00 a.m. Milton Bradley, the new FBI Director, will be doing the questioning, Andre' stated. He arranged with Anne to go with him in a limo with tinted windows to go to the FBI Building.

Arriving at the FBI Building, Anne didn't see any Militian characters she knew, was ushered right in with her attorney Andre' Knowles, and led to an interview room. A receptionist asked if Anne or her attorney would like any coffee or soda to drink. Anne said, this early. I'll have coffee with a bit of cream and two sugars, and the attorney said coffee black, no sugar. A registrar typist sat to the right of the director and a recorder sat on the desk, ready to record the interview. Waiting for the coffees, the FBI Director introduced himself and the registrar typist, and then Andre' introduced himself and his client, Anne Towers. The coffees arriving, they are ready to start.

Turning on the recorder, the Director stated, "This interview will be recorded, as a matter of record and any statements you give will be under oath, that you are telling the truth and the whole truth, leaving nothing out. Is that understood?"

"Yes, I understand that," replied Anne.

"Anne Towers has been given full federal immunity or full federal clemency on all federal and states' charges and given full federal witness protection in exchange for her testimony, right?" asked Andre' Knowles for the record.

"Yes, she been given full federal clemency on all charges, and 1 understand that goes for states' and local charges as well and with full federal witness protection; in exchange for her testimony. That is providing she hasn't committed any major serious or capital offenses and this time she is and has fully declared everything she ever committed or did illegally. And she tells everything she remembers and did for the Militias Militia Organization. Her testimony will have to be convening and compelling as well; that came from the U.S. Attorney General!" stated the Director. Andre' Knowles then nodded to Anne, okay.

"Now, state your full name, please, and raise your right hand." Her right hand raised, "Anne Marie Towers."

"Anne Marie Towers, do you swear to tell the truth, the whole truth, and nothing but the truth, leaving nothing out, so help you God?"

"I do."

"Then, let's begin. You have fully admitted to embezzling the Militias Militia Organization out of millions of dollars while you worked for them as an bookkeeper/accountant, is that correct?" asked the Director.

"Yes, that is correct," replied Anne. "I found out later on that it was the Militias Militia Organization, but when I first hired in the company I worked for was known as the 'Oasis Corporation. I am not aware of what their real product was, I just did my job as a bookkeeper/accountant, and I sensed early on that they did not appreciate it if I asked any questions about the company or their product. 1 was there to do my job and go," Anne taking a drink of coffee.

"They were that secretive? Didn't that arouse suspicion about the company and their business?" asked Milton Bradley, curious

"Yes, it raised a lot of suspicion, but with the pay I was getting. I felt I could afford to keep my mouth shut and mind my own business, just do my job and go home." "Oh, I chat with a few maintenance and utility workers and two office clerks there, but not about the business or the associates, or anything like that. The associates, clients and other business people kept their distance and I knew to keep my distance as well. I liked the excellent pay they were giving me and I didn't want to lose that." Anne replied, drinking her coffee.

"You are telling me you did not pick up or overhear any bits of information or anything said: you did your job, chat with two office clerks and a few maintenance and utility workers, that was it?" asked Milton Bradley, suspicious. 'You are under oath, so you must tell the truth!"

"I am telling the truth, that was it, I had my own office and no associates, clients or business people came in my office: just my boss to give me my check or tell me something to do, connected with bookkeeping and accounting. The office clerks came in to chat once or twice a day. The dockworkers did not come in my office. Trying to overhear or 'pickup' something would have cost me my job!"

"I believe that answers that question," Anne's attorney declared.

"I want to make sure that is all there was. She has held out on telling everything to Captain Hilary but you don't do that to me!'

"I am not holding out on anything, that was the extent of it! I did my job and went home. The associates, clients, and dockworkers kept their distance, too far for me to hear. To even try to hear would cost me my job!"

"The pay must have been good, they paid you to mind your own business and do your job, and you dared not to get nosey? How much did they pay you each week, or month? They must have paid you well!"

"I received $500.00each week, plus cost-of-living, plus 4 weeks paid vacation per year, and with health insurance coverage. I did not know of any other company that paid like that, I felt I could afford to mind my own business and just do my job, then go home. I didn't stare, study or analyze the associates or clients either, that would have been a real serious no-no and raised suspicions!"

"When did you learn or figure out that they were an illegal organization, how did you find that out if you weren't to be nosey or talk to anybody?" Bradley quizzed on, curious.

"About four years after I had worked there, some of the characters looked like well-heeled manicured thugs and killers, always well-dressed but their facial expressions gave them away arousing my suspicion, just a few of them but it was enough to confirm my suspicions, I then begin to take notice of what was in their accounts payable/receivable and the names of corporations more so than before, I knew the company was a 'front,'" Anne replied, finishing her coffee.

151

"What made or caused you to come to the decision to embezzle them of their money? How much money did you embezzle them for, a lot I suppose? Weren't you afraid to try something like that?" asked Milton Bradley, a bit puzzled. "You were afraid to be nosey but brave enough to embezzle them?"

"I took them for one hundred million dollars, and yes, I was scared. I realized that if I embezzled them of the money, they would come after me but they could not prosecute or even file charges because they were already illegal themselves. I realized it would have to be all completed and transacted in one big move all on the same day. Otherwise, they would be wise to what I was plotting and onto me. I waited for a year, planning and just being a good little worker."

"You did take them alright; you up and skipped town immediately the same day, I suppose. How did you know how to transfer that much money and where to transfer it?"

"I checked with different foreign offshore banks in countries with no extradition treaties. I got it all set up and then transferred it the next third week day. I knew to do it, I had to do it then, be ready to leave immediately on my lunch period. I already had everything packed and ready to leave immediately."

"You were a slick one, but they caught on after you didn't come back to work more than likely. When did you embezzle them and transfer this money to offshore banks?" Bradley quizzed.

"About two and half years ago. I don't remember the exact date, around sometime in June, I think. The date wasn't important to me then, just getting the money transferred and getting away before they found out and killed me!" Anne replied, nervous at thinking about it.

"But you remember the names of clients and associates in the bookkeeping and accounting?" Bradley asked, curiously and wondering.

"Yes. I remember their names because they kept coming across the accounts so often and I recorded them. I wasn't all tensed then; whereas I was transferring the money and moving in a hurry to get away. I didn't have time to be tensed and nervous, that would have slowed me down. Just the thought of it makes ME nervous, if they had caught me, it would have been goodbye Anne Towers! I have a list of their names and dates as close as I can remember them," Anne hands the Director the list of names and some "around-about" dates. The Director is stunned looking at the list.

"Would you sign and date this list, please?" Anne signs her name on the list and writes the day's date.

"You are sure about this list of names, you are absolutely certain of them?" The Director still looking at the list is in shock.

"Yes, I saw their names a good number of times. I just can't remember all of the dates, and the dates on there are close to being exact. Those names, I remember. I do not mean to destroy lives, but I remember those names; surprising, isn't it?"

"Yes. I would say so," replied Milton Bradley, still amazed at the names on the list

"You recognized three people as associates of the Militias Militia, correct?"

"Yes, they were associates of the Militias Militia, but I didn't know their role they had or position in the organization, until Captain Hilary told me. I knew not to ask, or else they would regard me with suspicion and wonder why I was asking. I would be risking my job and my life as well."

"All of this is true: you are not adding to or leaving anything out in this interview, are you? You are sure about all of these names on the list. You are sure about the information you have given," asked Milton Bradley, pressing to see if Anne would recant on anything she had said or change anything.

"No. I am not adding to or taking anything out or withholding anything. Those names on the list that I gave you, I remember those names in the accounts payable/receivable, as many times they showed up in the accounts. The dates are as close as I can remember. The information I have given you is actual truth," looking the Director in the eye. Anne wonders if some of those names are his friends, she suspects they are, the way he keeps asking and pushing. Is he a sympathizer? Anne wonders. If he is, I may be in danger!

"Now, the blackmailing of a person you caught embezzling his company's money and cheating on his wife, you admitted to the blackmailing fully and completely?"

"Yes. I have confessed to the blackmailing of him fully and completely."

"You realize you were supposed to report him to the authorities and let us deal with him?" pushed Bradley.

"Yes. I realize that, but I decided to punish him myself; he had and knew some powerful and sharp attorneys. Besides, back then, I could use the money," replied Anne.

"What did you do with the money? It was not your place to punish him, that is for the law and we have powerful and sharp attorneys as well!"

"I used it to improve my living standard, you may have sharp attorneys, but I felt would be a toss-up as to who would win!" Anne shot back.

"That is still for the law to deal with him! How much did you take him for?"

"I demanded $100,000 and he paid it, he would have lost more than that in a divorce and he knew it!"

"That is it. The total amount you blackmailed him for?" Bradley continued driving and pushing Anne. "Whether he wins or loses his shirt in a divorce does not matter, you should have reported him!"

"Yes, that was it, the total amount."

"You realize you will be testifying at the grand jury inquiry and the federal trial as well, as part of the full federal clemency and full federal witness protection deal?"

"Yes, I realize I will be testifying at the grand jury inquiry and the federal trial, in exchange for full federal clemency and full federal witness protection," stated Anne Towers for the record.

"You realize the defense attorney or attorneys will be questioning you as well as the District Attorney?"

"Yes, I realize both the defense attorneys and the District Attorney will be questioning me."

"Well that is it for now, I may need to question you further again later as well if I come up with more questions or anything new comes to light," the Director stated. "It would not be good if I find out you are still withholding information or leaving something out."

"I have told you everything I can remember and did. I am not withholding anything or leaving anything out," stated Anne.

"Okay for now then."

"Just get in touch with Captain Hilary and me as well if you wish to further question Anne Towers," stated Andre' Knowles. "Because of the attempts on Anne Towers and Rex Morgan, they stay in hiding and keep in contact with Captain Hilary."

"I see. I will get in touch with Captain Hilary and you then," the Director said and then shut off the recorder. The registrar typist got up and left, carrying the typewriter with her to record an FBI record.

"You are afraid to let him know where you are staying and hiding out?" the Director asked, puzzled.

"Yes, the last time Captain Hilary was supposed to be the only one to know where we were staying, we almost got killed. I am paranoid now and 1 think Rex might be too, a little but he is not letting on. I met my attorney at a location, so even he doesn't know where we are. I also found a mole inside their precinct and Captain Hilary found one later."

"Really, there were two moles in the Captain Hilary's precinct? Well, I can't blame you after all that has happened. I have heard that Rex has had same awful narrow escapes. The hit and run and the shooting at here; and now the shooting at the motel. But how are we supposed to know if you have been killed or kidnapped?"

"We're playing it close, by ear, if we see or hear anything that evens looks or sounds suspicious, or a bit questionable, we move immediately! The close calls are why we're not telling anyone where we are," stated Anne.

With that said, Anne Towers and her attorney, Andre' Knowles leave, Milton Bradley watching. Andre' drops Anne off on a corner and she quickly catches a ride with a cab to get out in the middle of traffic at a red light, and then quickly grabs another cab to go the other way and get out at a red light in the middle of traffic. From there, she walks a short distance to Rex and their undisclosed room.

"Well, how did it go?" asked Rex, anxiously.

"It was a bit rough, he kept pushing to get me to recant or change what I said, or get confused. He kept asking if I was sure of the names on the list I made out, makes me wonder if some of them are his friends or relatives. Wouldn't that be something if some of them were relatives!" Anne replies with a smirk. "He asked three or four times if I was sure about the names."

Rex looks in amazement and wondering, another mole in the FBI?

"Next is the questioning by the Assistant District Attorney, grand jury inquiry and then the federal trial, unless Milton Bradley has more questions for me," Anne stated. "I'm on a countdown, hopefully."

"I have heard that the grand jury inquiry and the federal trial can be the 'fun' part," stated Rex. "That depends on what you call 'fun' and where you are sitting," replied Anne sourly.

"I agree with you there," replied Rex, but then it will be over." (Anne interrupts to say "Really?") "You can move on with your life within the federal protection. "Or can we, I should say," Rex looking at Anne hopefully but wondering.

"I hope so. I hope so," sighed Anne hopefully.

Anne arrives with her attorney, Andre' Knowles for the questioning by the Assistant District Attorney, Cheryl Nickles. Andre' introduces himself and Anne. Cheryl introduces herself, and then turns on the recorder.

"Anne Towers will receive full federal clemency or immunity and full federal witness protection in exchange for her testimony, correct?" the attorney asked for the record.

"Yes, she will receive full federal clemency or immunity and full federal witness protection in exchange for her full testimony and providing she has not left anything out, added to or withholding anything: and she has not committed any serious or capital offenses. However, her testimony must be convincing and effective! That came from the U.S. Attorney himself" declared Cheryl Nickles. "I received a copy of the tape interview of you, Anne Towers with the FBI Director, Milton Bradley. Raise your right hand, please," Cheryl requested.

"Do you swear everything you told the FBI Director, Milton Bradley on that tape is true, nothing but the truth, and you left nothing out of this or added to, so help you God?"

"I do, the whole truth, nothing but the truth with nothing left out or added to, so help me God," stated Anne, her right raised.

"Then, let us begin. Well, I feel the need to review the same questions Melton Bradley asked you to get you to confirm your answers. The list of names you gave him is alarming!" Cheryl questioned Anne for another three hours, reviewing the recorded tape of Anne's interview with Milton Bradley and the list of names, adding a few extra questions.

"Is this it? it is over until the grand jury inquiry and the federal trial?" asked Andre'.

"Yes, unless I think of something or something new comes up; as for now, yes," replied Cheryl Nickles. "If you need to contact Anne for anything, contact captain Hilary and me," stated Andre' Knowles.

"Yes, Milton Bradley told me of your setup of contact and the two moles in the precinct... I guess I can't blame you."

Andre' Knowles and Anne Towers leaving and Anne arriving safely back at the place where she and Rex are staying, Anne feels relieved, but a slight headache. Now to wait for the arrival day of the grand jury inquiry if the sniper does not get me first, get this finished! Anne wonders what it will feel and be like after the federal trial is over and there is no more questioning or grilling! Where will I be living and what type of career or job will I have? It might be better to get some little minor job for a year or so, maybe the Militia will not think of that, hopefully! Rex feels better that so far, it is over until the grand jury inquiry and the federal trial, and then it will be finished, hopefully!

As the day approaches for the grand jury inquiry, Anne gets more nervous realizing there is a sharp shooter sniper out there somewhere, waiting. The District Attorney suggested that Anne being good at disguising herself, make herself look like a young juvenile delinquent cuffed to four female officers looking the same way going for arraignment until they get inside the court building, then she can change to look herself. They will arrive in a police van under armed guard. Hilary says that is a brilliant idea, the sniper won't recognize her, hopefully. When Rex calls Hilary, he tells Rex the District Attorney's idea of Anne disguising herself to arrive at the court house with four officers disguised as juveniles themselves. Rex tells Anne the suggestion and she feels she might be okay that way, if a sniper doesn't get close enough to see through the disguise.

"Have her to put on some make up, add a mole to her face, and add some facial sores or facial disfiguration," suggested Hilary. "We'll try to keep spectators at a distance and under watch, in case there is a sniper among them."

"Good idea, she will need all the precautions you can think of and come up with," Rex replied. Hilary tells Rex of faxing the Oriental's face and name to Jan Roberts and Harold Jabot, to let them put him in the news to see if anybody recognizes him or knows where he is. Rex tells Hilary he might find him if the Militia doesn't get to him first. Rex relaying this to Anne, she feels some relief and feels she might have a chance of survival past the grand jury and federal trial. Maybe, as the grand jury draws closer, Mitch Miller, Barry Williamson and the 3 Militia celebrities become anxious and nervous, knowing a sniper is waiting and watching. The District Attorney promised that they are taking every possible precaution diligently for their safety, but they wonder if that is enough to avoid a sniper's bullet. Word has leaked out that some congressional representatives, both national and state are on the list that Anne gave the FBI passed on to the District Attorney, and to the U.S. Attorney General. U.S. Senator Dural Bronson decides it is time to take a long vacation, shedding all the papers he has on file and deleting everything on computer and wrecks his hard-drives beyond repair. The shredded file papers he takes to the incinerator during the lunch period. Going back to his office, he packs up his perm things and leaves for home to pack his bags and disappear. Before leaving he transfers his savings and funds to a bank in Brazil, and then destroys his home computer. Being divorced with no children, he has nothing to hold him back.

U.S. Representative Hal Streader quickly writes his resignation and puts it in his congressional mailbox after deleting all of his files on computer and then shedding his desk files; and to take to the incinerator as well. His insurance paid up, leaving his wife and two sons as beneficiary; his family would feel disgraced and disown him, being he was third generation of U.S. congress representatives. He goes home and gets a bottle of sleeping pills and painkillers, drives to an old cottage he used go to relax and unwind for the last time. Hiding his car behind the cottage, he goes inside, swallows both bottles of pills, and lies on the couch.

Rex and Anne nervously enjoy the time they have left together before the grand jury inquiry begins, not knowing what lies ahead. Captain Hilary nervously goes about his daily routine, waiting until the grand jury starts up, worrying about Rex and Anne's safety, being that there is a sharp shooter out there waiting and watching, realizing Rex and Anne will be moving somewhere and ending the friendship between himself and Rex. Barry Williamson, Mitch Miller, and the three Militia celebrities arrested at a Samoa's, nervously and weary wait for their day before the grand jury, wondering what lies ahead. The maximum-security facility is on 'lockdown' until after the federal trial is over and finished, and the prisoners relocated to secure maximum-security prisons.

The District Attorney's Office is wrapping up and getting together everything they will be taking to the grand jury, and reviewing it carefully. The FBI and District Attorney's Office has found nothing or heard anything about the sniper; but everybody suspects the sniper is watching and waiting...

Anne goes to a pay phone to call her parents and sister to talk to them, not knowing if this will be the last time or not. Rex calls to check on his father. Now to wait for the day of the grand jury to begin, this will be very soon now.... Rex contacts Hilary to arrange for Sgt. Judy to receive Anne's expensive clothes and jewelry, going into hiding and a different lifestyle; she will have to give her expensive clothes and jewelry away. Hilary telling Judy; she is surprised, but understands and is thrilled. She is saddened at the thought of Rex going away as well. Hilary realizing Rex and Anne are preparing to disappear after the grand jury and federal trial, feels a sharp heartburn and a migraine coming on.

Anne after much thought, sits Rex down to discuss their situation, Rex is not a target of the Militia whereas she is and will continue to be for the rest of her life. For Rex to give up his life-long career would be a tremendous sacrifice that he has worked so hard for; and his best days are behind him in starting a new career. Anne feels he should stay here in Berkeley after the grand jury and the federal trial are over. Anne feels she might have to stay in hiding and maybe be on the run for some years. Rex is surprised at Anne saying this, but feels she might be right; the Militia would be after her for some years after the grand jury and federal trial. He could stay here and keep his career, but he would more than likely never see her again. This grieves Rex, but if he moved with Anne and started over, he would be doing it just to be with her if they could make a good relationship together.

"Are you absolutely sure about this, you feel this is best?" asked Rex, stressed but feeling she is right.

"As much as it grieves me. I feel it is the right and only choice, you have worked too hard to give up your career. Just stay with me until the federal trial is over and done with," asked Anne.

"Oh, I would do that, you need moral support and someone to talk to, and to watch your back," stated Rex. "Hilary would be happy to hear that!"

"Judy would be too," Anne replied, grinning. Rex laughing said, "Yeah, she would."

"I'll still give her my expensive clothes and jewelry, in changing my lifestyle for some years."

"Let us enjoy what time we have together then." Anne agrees.